Pride Publishing books by Xenia Melzer

Demon Mates
Demon's Wish
Demon's Game

Demon Mates

DEMON'S GAME

XENIA MELZER

Demon's Game
ISBN # 978-1-83943-770-0
©Copyright Xenia Melzer 2022
Cover Art by Erin Dameron-Hill ©Copyright January 2022
Interior text design by Claire Siemaszkiewicz
Pride Publishing

DEMON'S GAME

Dedication

To Paul — because Parker didn't want to be
acknowledged.
And to the wonderful person who went through
the trouble of playing the Iron Bull romance in
Dragon Age: Inquisition and uploaded it on
YouTube. You sparked the idea for Demon Wars!

Author's Note

Dear Readers,
In this book, I make use of voodoo lore because Jon's
Grann is a voodoo witch. The way I portray voodoo
has nothing to do with the actual religion and
everything to do with making it fit into my Demon
Mates universe — which, as many of you have noted in
the reviews, doesn't follow the usual rules for
demons, either. The voodoo in the story is not an
accurate representation of the religion and the cultural
idiosyncrasies. I gave Google Translator a run for its
money to get words and phrases in Haitian Creole,
and I tried to find traditional Creole names for my
characters to give the story more depth. I do not
intend to portray the culture in any way, shape or
form.

Prologue

A hundred and three years ago

In hindsight, dying had been easier than coming back from the dead. Living as an undead person was an entirely different matter and a lot more difficult than opening one's eyes again after they had presumably closed forever — but dying itself was easy. Jon didn't like to remember the days of agony that had led to his death, because he could have done without them, thank you very much. Perhaps that was the reason he welcomed death. Living had become much too painful.

The Spanish flu had swept through New Orleans like a tidal wave, taking with it not only the poor, but instead killing indiscriminately. Before the Reaper, all people were equal, a thought less comforting than Jon had hoped. As the estranged son of a famous doctor, Jon had had the advantage of knowing a thing or two about diseases, but no amount of care could battle the cramped living conditions in a poor house, not to mention the utter lack of hygiene. He'd ended up in one of the fabric halls they had turned into emergency hospitals, quickly succumbing to the virus. His malnourished body had fought for three days — at least that was what he remembered before it had given out and peace had come. *No pain. No screams. No fever. No hallucinations. Blessed silence and darkness.*

Until a voice had cut through it.

Mwen sipliye ou, Papa Legba, mennen sèvitè fidèl ou a tounen nan kò a.

Jon's Haitian Creole wasn't the best — though better than the nonexistent version his stuck-up family didn't speak — but he was fairly sure it meant something along the lines of *I beg thee, Papa Legba, bring back your faithful servant to the flesh.*

He wondered about that, since he didn't believe that he'd ever been a faithful servant to anybody, because he didn't like to answer to other people, which was something else his father did not look favorably upon. Then there was a creaking sound, as if cheap wood was being moved aside, scraping over more cheap wood along the way. It made Jon wonder where exactly he was, and he felt a panic attack rising when he realized he was currently lying in a flimsy wooden box he was able to identify as a coffin. Had they stuffed him in there without checking to see if he was truly dead? *How sloppy!* If he had to die of the Spanish flu under horrible circumstances, he felt he was at least entitled to people making sure he was dead before placing him inside a coffin.

Outside, the voice continued, now interrupted by another one.

"Are you sure this is working, Amede? We've been chanting for *hours*." The voice sounded like that of a professional whiner. Jon could instantly relate. Anything that required repetition for hours was probably not worth it.

"We haven't been here for *hours*, Gaspar. I'd say it was no more than thirty minutes." This voice was impatient, if with the whiner or because whatever they were doing didn't work, Jon wasn't sure.

"Thirty minutes is half an *hour*," the whiner, Gaspar, huffed. "I get it, Amede, I really do. I miss her as well, but face it, she's dead. She's an ancestor now."

"I don't care! We need her. Grann is the only one left. We need a priestess. I'm not ready to take on the mantle." The sheer despair in the voice woke feelings of pity in Jon. The conversation also distracted him from the fact that he was still in a coffin so cheaply made that he could feel the splinters digging into his back — which really shouldn't be his main priority at the moment. What he also realized was that splinters had a way of *becoming* a priority when they were poking into your flesh.

"You're doing it now, Amede. Killing a cock, drawing symbols with his blood and begging Papa Legba to bring Grann back. That's priesting."

A dead cock? Eww. Jon cringed. He'd never been good with blood, much to his father's dismay.

"And I'm *not* doing it right! Otherwise, she'd be awake by now!" Amede, the wannabe priest, sounded hysterical now.

The scraping sounded again, then a clattering, probably a coffin lid falling to the ground, Jon guessed. Two gasps and a collective, "Grann!" More shuffling, the sound of clothes catching on splinters and ripping, then a slap, another one, followed by two *Ouch!* and the stern voice of a woman.

"What did I tell you about raising the dead, *enbesil yo*?"

"Uh, you said to never do it?" Jon was sure that was Amede, his voice no longer hysterical but that of a child facing punishment for stealing the cookies from the jar, yet, at the same time, immensely relieved to have been caught.

"Exactly. And why do you think I said it?"

"Because it's dangerous?" Gaspar had obviously broken the jar and knew it.

There was a huff. "Dangerous doesn't even begin to describe it. And you did it in a room full of corpses!" Two more slaps followed, administered with enough force that Jon winced in his own coffin. He was starting to understand, though, and he didn't like what his brain was trying to explain to him.

"Let's see how much damage you caused. *Dakò*, is there anybody in here who has been woken by my grandsons' blabbering?" The female sounded all business-like and very commanding. Jon decided it was better to not contradict her by hiding. He couldn't be sure if she wouldn't start searching all the coffins. In fact, she sounded like somebody who never left a job half done, and if she did inspect them, he just knew he wouldn't like being found.

"Uhm, I'm here, though I'm not sure where *here* is exactly."

"Don't you worry, *mezanmi*. You just keep making some noise and my two idiot grandsons will have you out in no time at all."

Since he didn't know what to say, Jon decided hitting the coffin lid with his fist was a good compromise. He must have been quite to the back because it took some serious shuffling, cursing and thumping until he felt his coffin being moved, presumably to the ground. One particularly large splinter lodged itself firmly in his lower back when Amede and Gaspar put his coffin down quite carelessly. Jon couldn't suppress a whine, even though there was no real pain, as he realized with amazing clarity. He could feel the splinter, it wasn't nice, but there wasn't pain, per se—more something along the lines of pressure he knew to associate with pain.

A barked order in Creole cut through the air, and the next moment, the lid of his coffin broke and was lifted off. Jon blinked into the dim light of a room with a high ceiling, which had been white a long, long time ago. He could only see part of it because there were three faces staring down on him. Two belonged to young men, not older than he, both of them looking guilty as hell. The third was that of a woman who had lived a long and rich life, filled with lots of laughter if the web of wrinkles around her eyes was anything to go by. She was dead, just like him, though Jon didn't know how he knew. There was something about her, about the way she moved—or not moved, really—that told him she must be Grann. She extended her hand to him. Without thinking, he gripped it and let himself be yanked out of the coffin.

"My name is Batilda Honoré, former witch queen of New Orleans." She looked at her grandsons. "And apparently the new witch queen as well."

The two young men flinched under her stare. Jon looked around. They were in some kind of storage room, filled with rows and stacks of coffins. All of them were shut, which meant they were occupied. He suppressed a shudder. There was a reason he had refused to follow in his father's footsteps. To distract himself, Jon bowed his head to Batilda.

"It's a pleasure to meet you, Mrs. Honoré. I'm Jon Levard."

She smiled at him and patted his cheek. "It's Batilda for you…or Grann. I have a feeling it will be Grann very soon. You must be quite confused, Jon. I can assure you that I'm going to do my best to help you adjust to your new situation."

Jon furrowed his brows. He knew the stories about zombies. "Am I your slave?"

"No, sweet boy, no, you're not. For you to be a slave to anybody's will, these two *enbesil* would have needed to perform a very different ritual." The glare she sent the two young men had them literally backing away from her. "We don't do that, because people generally don't like it when their loved ones or members of their community are forced to give up their eternal rest, and *we* don't like being chased with pitchforks and burned at the stake. Win-win." Her smile was still bright, but something in her eyes told Jon not to follow this topic any further.

"What am I then?" It was a valid question in his opinion. While he was standing there, talking to Batilda, he had noticed how much sharper his hearing had become, how keen his eyesight suddenly was and how his surroundings seemed to be more real than when he had still been alive. It wasn't bad, just very strange.

Batilda patted his cheek again, reminding him of his own gran, who had passed more than five years before. "You, my boy, are a blessing, a miracle, a gift from Papa Legba. I don't know why he chose to wake you as well, but here you are. *Wi*, call me Grann already, because you are definitely family now."

And just like that, Jon had become an honorable Honoré and gained not only a Grann but also a huge family with countless cousins, aunts and uncles, as well as an endless stream of ancestors. It was the family he knew he'd never needed but had to deal with anyway, because they wouldn't go away...*ever.*

Chapter One

Present day

"I still think it would be better if you came home, *ma cheré*. I don't like you being so far away." Grann sounded worried through the phone, and Jon felt bad about that—not bad enough to return home to New Orleans, but bad enough to try to placate her.

"I'm happy here, Grann, I swear. Sammy is a fantastic landlord and friend, and I have my book club."

"I know. I've seen it." There was a pregnant pause that Jon knew better than to disturb. "The pictures I'm getting now are all blurred, though, and the *zanset yo* are restless. They don't know what to make of the situation."

Jon suppressed a sigh. It was the same problem as always—or the same two problems. The first one he could address easily enough, even if his words didn't have a lot of impact on either Grann or the ancestors.

Come to think of it, that was the case with everything he did since he'd moved from New Orleans to Beaconville some five years before. And he was getting distracted.

"I already told you that Dre is super nice and also Sammy's mate. He would never harm me."

"*Wi, wi,* I know. I can see the threads of his love for his mate and everybody and everything his mate holds dear. It's the *only* thing I can see clearly."

"I told you... I asked Dre and he's not doing it on purpose."

"He doesn't have to." Grann's voice had taken on a dark quality, a tone she usually reserved for everything occult she thought Jon wasn't ready for or strong enough to hear. "He's chaos personified. It's his natural state. I wonder how your witch friends cope with it."

Jon thought of Maribel and Mavis, the two witches in their book club. "I think Mavis once mentioned it to Dre shortly after he and Sammy had become mates. He said to give the magic some time, and they haven't complained since."

"I see." Grann was mulling this over, shortly side-tracked by the magical possibilities Jon would never understand. Like a heat-seeking missile, though, she returned her attention to the matter at hand. "You really don't want to come back home? Just yesterday I saw the obituary for a Silvery Sugar Fox. I could wake him for you, and I would, to make you happy."

Jon rolled his eyes. He knew Grann meant well — the whole family, alive and dead, did — but Jon had finally drawn the line when Grann and the others had started mentioning obituaries like they were the last rave in dating sites. Funnily enough, they hadn't batted an eye when he'd told them he was gay, after having lived with them for more than ten years, long enough for them to become his new family, one he dearly loved, even if they annoyed the ever-loving hell out of him sometimes. Coming out to them back in 1932 had been terrifying, but he hadn't been able to keep lying to them and himself any longer.

It had taken them fifteen more years to decide he should start looking for a husband, and they had managed to be relatively subtle about it—casually mentioning deaths of eligible men over breakfast and, in the case of the ancestors, sending him dreams of newly deceased men—until the Internet had taken on steam in the nineties. Subtlety had died like a roach under the heel of a vicious housewife then.

First, they had tried to set him up with the living, presumably to get him into the swing of things, whatever that was supposed to mean. Jon just couldn't do it. He had gotten used to not being alive, had arranged himself with the prospect of seeing eternity if he so desired. He was also comfortable with his enhanced abilities that didn't make him cool and smooth like a were-creature or a vampire but were enough to distinguish him from humans, thus making it impossible for him to go out with one of them.

What he couldn't stand—not to this day—was feeling the warmth of another being while he himself was always cold. It was a brutal reminder how he shouldn't be there anymore, even though Grann had assured him that Papa Legba always had a plan for whatever he did. If said plan included having Jon living celibate, it had worked. His sex drive had apparently not woken with him. He still could appreciate masculine beauty, and he even knew what he would want in a man, *if* he would want a man. It was a strange state of being, caught between wanting intimacy and not being able to pursue it, made even worse by his family's meddling. For some time, he had thought he might be asexual, but while he was still alive, his sex drive had been a prominent part of his life and he didn't think his sexual orientation had changed with death.

After he had finally gotten it into his family's thick skulls that a living man wasn't what he was looking for, not even for the sake of sowing his wild oats, they had swung back to their initial MO and the thing with the obituaries had taken on new momentum.

Jon had dealt with it as best as he could, aka ignoring his family by keeping himself busy with staying on top of every new computer development and diving deep into the world of video games, making himself a part of their evolvement from Pong to Space Invaders to Pac-Man. From there it went on with SimCity, Final Fantasy and Castlevania in the second half of the eighties. By the time real-time strategy games like Dune II or Warcraft: Orcs and Humans started their triumphal march in the nineties, Jon was already a veteran in the scene and a sought-after game tester and advisor for all the huge companies. Strictly speaking, he was several veterans, because being a zombie meant he would be around long enough for people to notice, so he took some precautions until he realized that nobody in the gaming business gave a damn about suspicious longevity, because people simply assumed the person behind the alias, in his case PLM—Papa Legba's Miracle—changed while the alias stayed on. He'd been PLM ever since, abandoning his other virtual personalities. He was proud to say his name was linked to quite a few legends in the world of gaming, and his fame was paying off nicely. It also helped him to bury the confusing feelings he was having regarding his life under an avalanche of pretend worlds where reality was simply a nuisance.

But no matter how deeply he immersed himself in the world of virtual reality, no matter how much money he gave Grann and the family to prove to them what a successful and fulfilled undead life he was leading, they wouldn't stop poking their noses into his business, namely his nonexistent love life.

One day, Jon had had enough. He'd hung a map of the US on a wall, taken a dart and thrown it. He'd never heard of Beaconville before, but that had been where he'd be living from then on. After much complaining and endless discussions about how the Midwest was too far away from New Orleans and that the snow would kill him, not to mention what he did to his poor family, leaving them behind, Grann finally caved and gave her blessing. Because she was the undisputed matriarch, nobody dared contradict her, and some of his younger cousins even helped him move his stuff to the only hotel in the small town, 'M&M's B&B'. Meeting Mavis and Maribel had been a stroke of luck, the witches immediately knowing what he was. They'd introduced him to Sammy, who was open and friendly without being nosy and who happened to have an empty basement he didn't know what to do with. It was perfect, and until the incident where he'd forgotten to eat some brain and his body had reminded him loudly how important that was everything had been fine. Luckily for him, Sammy didn't spook easily and had managed to distract him with some leftover apple pie while he'd made a dash for the butcher to buy Jon a whole pig brain.

After that, he'd gotten another call from Grann, telling him in no uncertain terms that if he didn't take better care of himself, she would personally drag him back to New Orleans and Mavis and Maribel had explained to him that he needed to get out at least once a month for his 'mental hygiene', as they called it. Jon was well versed in understanding subtext, the message being he would be playing with way less than a full deck of cards if he didn't start forming some bonds outside his virtual realities.

Sammy had just started his book club, which seemed as good a reason as any to come up for air from his beloved basement. By now, Jon wouldn't miss the regular meetings with his friends and he even left the basement once a week to chat with Sammy or Milo in the bookstore. When Dre was there, they would read mangas together on one of the couches Sammy had renovated, while they drank hot chocolate or Frappuccino's.

Jon thought he was making great progress regarding his social life, while Grann thought it was time for him to come back home, which was the other bone they regularly discussed heatedly.

"It's Silver Fox *or* Sugar Daddy, Grann. And I want to get to know the man I'm hooking up with, which is difficult when he's already dead."

"Now you're just being stubborn." Grann chuckled. "Fine… I'll leave you to your games. Perhaps I'll wake him for myself. His picture does look good, and I could do with some action, *pa kwe*?"

"Grann! I don't need to hear that!"

"It's only natural, *cherie*. And just because *you* refuse to live—"

"I've heard enough. Do what you must, but leave me out of it. And don't tell me about it."

Now Grann was laughing out loud. "I love you, *cherie*. Take good care of yourself."

"I love you, too, Grann—and I will."

She hung up on him, leaving Jon wondering what she was cooking up in her brain to let him off the hook so quickly. Usually her rantings about him coming home lasted a lot longer. He shrugged, knowing he would find out sooner than he would like and determined to enjoy the time until the boot dropped on his head. He had a book club meeting about *The Witcher* to attend.

Chapter Two

Barion was pacing in front of his huge TV screen, waiting for Sammy to come out of his library. His older brother, Dresalantion — or Dre for short, and mate of Sammy — was lounging on the designer couch in his mansion in the Carpathians, eating a *tartuffone* he had just bought at his favorite gelateria in Rome, seemingly without a care in the world. Of course, he hadn't brought any for Barion, who had been watching Sammy for his brother — not that Sammy needed watching, at least not in the sense Dre thought.

The small human was peaceful enough, though with a knack for getting into interesting and potentially dangerous situations with paranormal beings. The way he had met Dre — as his sacrifice — was the argument Dre always brought up when either Sammy or Barion argued that he could take care of himself for a few hours. The human was also a menace when it came to books. Barion had a lot of them in his library and Sammy loved organizing them — at least that was what Sammy called it. Barion thought of it more along the lines of wreaking absolute havoc in the once-peaceful chaos that had been the books he'd accumulated throughout the years.

"Would you stop with the pacing, Barion? We still have time." Dre had chocolate and cocoa powder all around his mouth, contrasting with his deep red skin.

"I know we still have time. And your mate is using it to misplace every book in my library."

"You barely go there." Dre had a point, not that Barion would ever admit it.

"It's the principle of the thing. Besides, I can't find anything anymore!"

"You couldn't find anything before." Barion itched to wrap his claws around Dre's neck. That his brother was right didn't help his temper.

"But I knew where the books were *not!*" His tone was a shrill whine, even to his own ears. He really wanted some of that *tartuffone*. Damn his brother for being so inconsiderate.

"Do you listen to yourself sometimes, or is what's coming out of your mouth just stream of consciousness?"

"Fuck you, Dre. Now drag your mate out of my library. There's a book club we have to attend."

Dre got up slowly, his tall frame unfolding gracefully from the soft confines of the couch. Barion's eye for aesthetics was well-trained enough to appreciate what he was seeing—a very fine specimen of a royal demon, just like himself—even though his brother was testing his patience. Since he'd met his fated mate, Dre had become more of a family man and spending time with him and Sammy was actually fun. *Well, most of the time. When they don't mess up my books and refuse to bring me sweets from Italy.* "You do realize it won't start without Sammy because he's the host?"

Again with the logic. Barion *so* didn't need that. "Then get him!"

"Geez, why are you so keen on the book club all of a sudden? After the one time you've been there, you said it wasn't for you, even though we had so much fun telling all those stories about Lovecraft's demons. I thought you enjoyed yourself." The slight reproach in Dre's voice did nothing to soothe Barion's agitation.

"Yes, I did, but that was because there was something real behind the *Cthulhu Cycle*. It's not nearly as funny when I have to *read* the books. But this time, the topic is *The Witcher*."

"Which is also a book...or books." Dre furrowed his forehead, apparently not understanding the severity of what they would be discussing this time.

"And a video game, if not *the* video game — and a very successful TV series. Don't you get it, Dre? This is finally a topic I can relate to."

"You mean you can relate to a naked Henry Cavill in the bathtub." Dre was grinning broadly. Barion huffed.

"That too. He does look good for a human, you know."

"Who does look good?" Sammy was coming from the direction of the library, his bi-colored eyes lighting up when he saw his mate. "Oooh, you've got *tartuffone*."

"Yes, *mo grah thu, tartuffone*. You want some? And Henry Cavill looks good as the Witcher."

"He does. Why do you think everybody was so keen on involving the series in our discussion?" Sammy was pressing his slim body against Dre's side, eyeing the half-eaten treat in his mate's hands with pure lust.

With an indulgent smile, Dre handed it to him, not taking his eyes off Sammy's lips while he took the first bite. Barion had to avert his gaze so the two wouldn't see the jealousy in his eyes. He decided to make some gagging noises instead, to show clearly how much he didn't envy them their happiness...which he didn't. *No.* He was happy for his brother — *most* of the time.

"How about you eat your sweet at the shop, *mo grah thu*, where Barion can talk to the others and doesn't have to watch us." The amusement in Dre's voice was almost enough to gloss over the hint of worry Barion detected. He very pointedly stared at the wall. A sigh, then, "We'll see you at the store."

When Barion turned, Dre and Sammy were gone, the rift in time and space Dre had used to travel to Beaconville already closed. Barion took a few fortifying breaths, readying himself for meeting Sammy's and Dre's friends again. He had talked to them at the wedding party his brother had hosted after Sammy had become his mate, and they had been friendly enough. Still, Barion felt a little shy around them, seeing them as this homogenic group of book lovers who always had something to talk about, be it their mutual love of Jane Austen or *Foucault's Pendulum* by Umberto Eco, a novel they could argue about seemingly forever.

Barion wasn't a keen reader. He had a vague love for books as something that had to be preserved and respected, but his true interest was video games, hence his enthusiasm for this book club meeting's topic. It was the first time he felt he could contribute something besides a vast pool of ignorance. Plus, some stealthy questioning of his brother had revealed that Mavis and

Maribel would be providing the snacks for this meeting and their baking was superb, as Barion had found out at the wedding party. He drew himself up to his considerable height of eight feet, a little smaller than Dre, which never ceased to annoy him, and opened a rift in time and space to get to Sammy's bookstore in Beaconville. There was no need to glamour himself because the meeting was strictly paranormals, and Sammy's human shop assistant, Milo, knew about demons because he'd been the one to try to sacrifice Sammy to Dre — a long story and one Barion still wasn't sure what to make of.

He stepped into nothing to enter pandemonium — or so it seemed.

"And I'm telling you that Vision is still out there somewhere, waiting for Wanda to find him."

"You're such a romantic sap, Troy. He's dead, killed by Thanos. All that's left of him is in Wanda's mind."

"Then explain to me, Emilia, why they introduced White Vision to the show?"

"To keep up the hopes of people like you. What else?"

"People like *me*?"

Barion risked a glance around the stack of old wine crates where Sammy had displayed his latest manga purchases and saw Troy, the blond alpha werewolf, standing toe-to-toe with Emilia, the ancient vampire. Both of them were showing their fangs, which didn't seem to bother anybody. Sammy was over at the coffee machine with Dre, busy filling mugs, Amber, the banshee, was helping Declan, the other alpha werewolf, to arrange the delicious bakings of Mavis and Maribel on two huge plates while the two witches were cuddling on one of the couches, watching Troy and Emilia duke it out. There was growling involved by now.

"People who can't face harsh reality."

"You do know the Scarlet Witch and Vision have two children in the comics, don't you?" Troy was almost snarling. Emilia wasn't impressed.

"Children of the devil or whatever, not really theirs, as you may recall."

Troy threw his hands in the air. "There's no sense talking to you. You always assume the worst."

"Because that's what usually happens." Emilia was unflappable. "Believe me, Marvel is priming Wanda to become the ultimate villain."

"She's too sweet for that!" Troy looked as if he were only a second away from jumping at Emilia with his claws out.

"Man, don't you realize she's just yanking your chain? Emilia, stop bullying him. Troy's had a rough week." Declan sounded almost bored, as if violence wasn't imminent. Then again, from what Barion knew about werewolf culture, violence was *always* just a wrong word away with them, very much like it was with demons.

Emilia grinned broadly. "I was just trying to get him out of his funk."

"Thank you for your trouble, but as you can see, he's not receptive to your special brand of encouragement at the moment." Declan held out the plate with cookies, muffins and miniature apple pies to her and his fellow alpha. "Take some sugar, you two."

Both Emilia and Troy huffed before grabbing one of each treat, devouring them so fast that Barion started worrying about missing out.

"Don't be alarmed. They're always like this. I guess it's part of their charm."

Barion spun around to see who was talking to him. It was Jon, the zombie, the quietest of the group. He smiled at Barion, his brown eyes barely visible under the mop of unruly dark strands that fell to his shoulders.

"It's nice to see you again, Barion." Jon nodded at him, not offering his hand, a quirk Barion had already gotten explained at the one book club meeting he had attended, as well as at the wedding party. Apparently, the zombie didn't like feeling the warmth of other people, and demons ran hotter than everybody else. Barion nodded back, glad for this soft entry to meeting Sammy's closest friends again.

"It's nice to be here. I can't wait to talk about *The Witcher*."

Jon smiled broadly. "Me neither. It's such a broad field, what with the books and the games and the series. I'm so glad Sammy finally picked it up for the group. It will hopefully derail them from discussing Marvel to death."

"They do seem to take it quite seriously."

Jon rolled his eyes. "You think?"

He stepped around the crates and Barion followed, grateful for Jon taking the lead. Everybody greeted him warmly, the wariness he usually encountered from other paranormals completely missing.

Good thing they're already used to Dre. It makes it easier to strike up a conversation without sending everybody running away.

It had happened more than once to Barion. In fact, it happened so often that he had stopped trying to meet non-demons some three centuries before. Demons had a bad reputation—admittedly rightfully so, at least in many cases—and Barion had gotten tired of fighting against something he would never be able to change. Looking around the group while he sat down in the huge yellow beanbag chair next to Jon, who had chosen a cozy-looking armchair, Barion realized that finding a mate and adopting his friends was a good way of changing at least a few people's minds.

Dre had told him how opposed Mavis and Maribel had been to him dating Sammy, and looking at them happily joking with Dre, Barion had trouble believing the two sweet ladies had come to their first meeting with his brother with two baskets full of lethal spells. Once everybody was seated with their preferred beverage, Sammy clapped his hands and silence ensued.

"Welcome to you all. I'm so happy you could make it today." He smiled joyfully while Dre squeezed his thigh.

"Uhm, we usually make it." That was Amber, who was staring at Sammy with a confused look.

"Shh, he was just getting started." Emilia grinned at Amber. Sammy ignored them.

"As you may have already seen, we've got a guest today—Barion, Dre's younger brother. I'm sure you all know him from the wedding, and he's also been at the book club once before."

Barion nodded at each member of the club, getting friendly nods and some waves in return while pointedly ignoring the little jab about him not having become a regular member. He wouldn't let himself be shamed into reading when he didn't want to. He was too old for that.

"Barion is here because today we're discussing *The Witcher*, a topic so vast that I'm sure it will keep us occupied for at least three sessions." Sammy was now bouncing in his seat from sheer excitement. It was hard not to be infected by his eagerness. "Who wants to go first?"

There was a moment of silence before Emilia leaned forward, putting her huge mug with some Japanese green tea down on the coffee table in front of her. It was the one with Smaug and Drogon on it, two dragons that Barion loved.

"My family has strong ties to the Eastern European countries, and even though my Polish is a bit rusty, I enjoyed reading the books in the original language. I was especially drawn in by the world building, which is kind of similar to Tolkien and yet absolutely unique in its own right, full of references to Eastern European folklore, which I adore. I also liked the strong female characters in the book, Yennefer and Ciri and Triss, who I feel are the focal points for Geralt throughout the series. Everything he does somehow comes back to either one or all of them."

"I agree with you, though I think Geralt's relationship to Yennefer is written as a hyperbole. I mean, how tumultuous can the ties between lovers become?" Troy took another cookie and stuffed it into his mouth. The way he and Emilia smiled at each other had Barion wondering if he had imagined the whole *WandaVision* argument before.

"Very true. Perhaps it's even meant as a mockery for other famous fantasy pairs. I mean, Andrzej Sapkowski did include humoristic hints in his books, like the one about Thomas Edison." Maribel looked thoughtful.

"I wonder why relationships are so important." Amber sounded as if she were talking to herself, not addressing the rest of the group. It was Dre who answered her.

"I think it's because that's what most humans' lives are about—and those of most paranormals as well." He gave Sammy a soft kiss on the temple. "We're all looking for our special someone. It's at the core of our nature."

The others nodded, with the exception of Jon and Amber. The banshee still appeared as if she truly didn't understand, which was valid for an asexual creature whose sole experience with relationships was to tell heroes—and these days heroines as well, because banshees were all about going with the times—when they were going to die, and Jon looked simply sad. Suddenly driven by the urge to wipe the despair from Jon's face, Barion decided to throw in his two cents.

"I'm not sure relationships are really at the core of *The Witcher*, at least not when looking at the games. I admit they are just based on the books, not following them accurately, but the focus is on the decisions Geralt—or rather, the player—makes and all the possible outcomes of that, which I think aligns nicely with the premises of magic and chaos in the books. The decisions that shape the story."

"Ooh, yes, you're absolutely right." Jon was visibly perking up. "In *The Witcher III: Wild Hunt*, you've got thirty-six different endings to the story, depending on the decisions the player has made throughout the game. It's fascinating and always a surprise."

"Like the law of surprise." Barion grinned.

"Yeah, just like that. I mean, I've played the game fifteen times now and there's still possible outcomes I haven't seen. It's so much fun, especially with the crones of Crookback Bog and the Bloody Baron."

"Don't forget the Whispering Hillock Tree. I love that spirit." Barion couldn't contain the excited giggle escaping him. *This is so much fun!*

"I must admit I haven't killed him once yet. I *love* that horse." Jon sighed. "I'm afraid I'll have to do it soon if I want to see *all* the other outcomes."

"Have you tricked the spirit?"

"No, and that just feels like betrayal. I can't betray a beautiful horse like that, can I?"

"No, although, strictly speaking, at the time of betrayal it would still be a bloated spiky whatever." Barion shrugged.

"It's still wrong. Am I crazy for being attached to a virtual horse?" Now Jon sounded almost anxious.

"Have you seen the episode where Sheldon's WoW account is hacked?"

"They stole Glen, the battle ostrich! What a cruel thing to do." Jon shook his head about the perfidy of the World of TV series.

"Yeah. My point is, Sheldon loved that virtual bird, so why can't you be attached to a virtual horse?"

"You're right. Thank you, Barion. I do feel better now." Jon's smile was infectious.

"Uh, guys, I think we veered a little off-topic here." Sammy looked almost apologetic, while Dre and the two werewolves were silently laughing. Mavis and Maribel were making out and Emilia and Amber had their focus on the rapidly emptying trays with the treats.

"And it took less than ten minutes. That's a new record for us." Declan made a show of looking at his watch, a Rolex, if Barion wasn't mistaken. "Congratulations, guys.

I hereby name you the new Kings of Off-Topic." He bowed with a flourish, which would have been awkward with any other person trying to pull that off while still sitting, but werewolves probably didn't even know how 'awkward' was spelled. For them, only 'predatory grace' existed.

"We are honored to take the crown." Barion gave his own bow, which had the bean bag moaning under his weight. So much for 'predatory grace'. Well, if push came to shove, grace didn't keep you alive, while brute force did, and demons were the definition of power. *What have we been talking about?*

"When are we going to discuss naked Henry Cavill in the tub? I have to admit that watching the show was the most pleasant part of the homework for this session." Mavis winked while Maribel playfully swatted her arm.

"Shh, not in front of the children."

Troy rolled his eyes. "Please, if there was a chance to get a piece of Henry, Declan and I would even put up with having you two in that tub with us."

"I can't hear a thing…la, la, la!" Emilia was covering her ears with her hands.

"What about you, Sammy? Would you accept those four in the tub for the sake of Henry?" Barion couldn't keep a lid on his mischief, and seeing Dre bristling was *so* much fun. Sammy cocked his head, clear confusion written in his features.

"Why would I want a bathtub with Henry and the others when I can have a bed with only Dre in it?"

Dre stuck his tongue out at Barion before he proceeded with giving Sammy's tonsils some extra care.

So much for yanking Dre's chain.

"You two are disgusting." Barion mock shuddered.

"Ah, young love. So sweet." Mavis sighed, shamelessly ogling Sammy and Dre.

"And we're off-topic again." Amber snatched the last cookie, which had Barion diving for the second plate with the miniature apple pies. He would be damned if he didn't get at least one of them. It was an important lesson, though, not to get too caught up in the discussion while there was still food available. Paranormals were rabid eaters—and damn sneaky, too.

The banter continued for some time, with occasional discussions about *The Witcher* thrown in, and when it was time to say goodnight, Barion insisted on escorting Jon down to his basement. After the lively discussion, he felt a strange connection to the zombie, probably born of their mutual love of gaming. Barion was eager to make new friends, and Jon seemed like a good prospect. The zombie didn't protest when Barion followed him down into the well-lit cellar that had hardwood floors and walls that were painted a warm peach color. As cellars went, this one had managed to disguise itself as a beautiful apartment. Jon's living room was every gamer's dream. Barion stopped short on the threshold, his jaw almost hitting the floor.

"Wow. Just *wow*."

"You like it?" Jon seemed almost shy.

"What's not to like? You have, what? Four sixty-five-inch monitors, the most impressive surround system I've seen in a long time and, trust me, I know my way around them, an ergonomic chair with several lounge options, all the important gaming consoles and the perfect light. I'm tempted to move in with you."

Barion was sure Jon would have blushed if that were possible for zombies. "Thank you. I did my best with the interior."

"And you were a thousand percent successful." Barion looked around the room with the tasteful dragon mural on one wall—he would bring Dre his favorite ice cream daily for the next hundred years if the flames spilling from the dragon's mouth weren't glow in the dark—the strategically placed spotlights and the beautiful quilt in all shades of green on the ergonomic chair. It was a dream come true.

"Would you like to come play with me tomorrow? I was thinking about starting another round of *The Witcher III*."

Barion turned to Jon. "I'd love to. We could see what happens when we sacrifice the children. I haven't done that before."

"Me neither." Jon averted his gaze. "With you, I might be brave enough to try."

"It's a deal. When would you like me to come over tomorrow?"

Jon thought for a moment. "I have some work to do, but should be done around two p.m. Is that okay for you?"

"Whatever works for you, Jon. My schedule is pretty open, you know." For the first time in what felt like eons, admitting to his lack of meaningful things to do didn't bother Barion. On the contrary, he was grateful for it.

"Then I'm looking forward to seeing you tomorrow." Jon wrung his hands nervously. "I'm sorry, but I'm not very good at social interactions. I loved our discussion, though."

"It's fine. I'm a bit rusty myself." That was exaggerating, because the things Barion knew about modern social interactions would easily find room on his pinkie's nail. It seemed to soothe Jon, though, which was all Barion cared about. "See you tomorrow then." He lifted his hand, the claws extended, to rip into space and time.

"Tomorrow." Jon's shy smile followed Barion back home to his mansion.

Chapter Three

Jon was pacing nervously in his living room-gaming paradise. It was almost two p.m., and he wasn't sure if he was happy about Barion's upcoming visit or if he should hide until the demon was gone again. Inviting Dre's brother had been a spur of the moment thing, born out of the genuine pleasure Jon had felt while discussing *The Witcher* games with Barion. It was the first time he had spoken with somebody like-minded in real life, and the exhilaration about it had messed with his common sense. He was a zombie, a solitary creature. He didn't invite people randomly into his sanctuary. No, he didn't. Only, he *had* done it. Barion would come. He was sure of it.

Before Jon could work himself up even more, a tear appeared out of thin air, hovering right next to his two sub woofers, heralding Barion's appearance. A moment later the demon stepped through, his broad figure allowing Jon only a brief glance at the darkness from which he had come. Sammy had once told him traveling via time-space was quite boring once you got over the rush of being 'there' one second then 'here' the next, but Jon wasn't sure if something so awesome could ever get boring.

"Hi, Jon, I brought snacks." Barion held out a huge paper bag filled with all kinds of unhealthy sweets, from Snickers bars, gummy bears, Skittles and chips to salted peanuts and roasted cashews. Four bottles of Coke rounded out the perfect gaming sustenance.

"Thank you. We're going to need them." He gestured to the two armchairs he had prepared for their gaming afternoon. "Please, take a seat."

Barion stepped forward, scrutinizing the two seats. "Which one do you prefer?"

"I usually take my ergonomic chair, but since it isn't here, I have no preferences."

"Then I'll take the left one. My peripheral vision is better on the right." Barion was referring to the two screens Jon had arranged in front of the armchairs.

Once the demon had taken his seat and was reaching for the gaming console that Jon had placed on the low table between the two chairs, he put the snacks on it, making little heaps that could be easily accessed. The bottles of Coke went in the middle, where the danger of pushing them over in the heat of the moment was smallest.

"I see you've had to mop up spilled stickiness before." Barion grinned.

"It was terrible. I had to pause the game." Jon shuddered at the memory.

"We live and learn. I spilled it all over my keyboard. Had to get a new one."

"The horror! Did you have a spare?"

Barion looked at him as if he was offended by the question. "Of course, I had a spare. Who do you take me for?" Then his lips split into a huge grin. "Still had to change it out—which took forever—then I needed over thirty minutes to get my flow back."

"I hate it when that happens." Jon was done laying the snacks out and took his own seat. He activated his console and the screen lit up showing two windows, one from YouTube with a stream of comments coming in. Jon cursed inwardly for having forgotten to close the account. Barion saw it as well. He stared at the screen, then at Jon, then back at the account. Jon could practically see the gears turning in his head. Of course, a gamer like Barion would know what this was about.

"Don't tell me you're PLM."

"Don't tell me you know who PLM is." Jon tried to make a joke, failing completely.

Barion pulled himself up, his eyes glowing with enthusiasm. "Of course I know who PLM is—just the most popular YouTube game tester to ever set up an account. I have subscribed to your channel, and I try to follow all your live streams. You're awesome."

Jon didn't know what to say. He was bad with taking compliments, and Barion's glowing praise made him physically uncomfortable. He had started the channel partly out of boredom and partly because he wanted to try his hand in earning money that way. Never would he have expected to become some sort of Internet celebrity. If he had known, he would have never done it. Jon navigated the cursor to minimize the window.

"Let's just play, okay?"

"I'm not sure I can just play, knowing who I'm playing with." Barion grabbed a handful of roasted cashews and started munching. The rich aroma of nuts permeated the air, instantly soothing Jon with its familiarity.

"You can. It's still just me, Jon, the zombie living in your brother-in-law's basement." He paused. "Is that correct? Sammy being your brother-in-law? Or is there another term you'd prefer?"

"There is indeed another term I prefer for Sammy." Barion turned to him, the silver tattoos on his blue skin glowing in the semi-darkness Jon preferred when playing video games. "Pain in my ass."

The words took a moment to filter into Jon's brain, which was still occupied with how intricate the swirls on Barion's neck were, where they peeked out of his V-neck shirt. "I'll tell him you said that."

"He already knows. I explain it to him every time he reorganizes my library."

"Uh, I heard that differently. If I remember correctly, Sammy used the terms 'chaos', 'absolute mess', 'without rhyme or reason' and, I think, 'dilettante' in conjunction with you and your library."

Barion's lips twitched. "Yeah, according to him, the only reason he's not taking my books away is because he doesn't have enough room to store them." He leaned toward Jon, a conspiratorial gleam in his gorgeous black eyes. "To be honest, I think he needs the challenge."

Jon started laughing. Barion was so odd, in a good way. "I'm not going to contradict you on that. Sammy's always looking for something to occupy him. Now, let's get on with the game."

They started playing, happily discussing all the choices that could be made, commenting on the graphics and interludes, cursing their opponents and comparing possible outcomes after certain choices. Then it was time for the chapter with the crones and Jon's favorite quest, the Whispering Hillock Tree. As it turned out, Barion was just as enthusiastic about it.

Listening to the eerie voice of the tree spirit, Jon tried to decide which choice he should suggest. He hadn't lied when he'd said he couldn't bring himself to trick or even kill the tree spirit. Glancing to his left, he saw Barion staring intently at the screens.

"What should we do? I want to free him so badly, but I always do that." The demon's silver tattoos were glowing, a sign for his agitation, as Jon had learned from Sammy.

"I want to free him as well. The horse is so gorgeous."

"But then we'll never learn if there's a different outcome if we kill him." Barion sounded as torn as Jon felt. They both reached for their Cokes, needing sugary reinforcement in the face of such an impossible choice.

"You know what? To hell with it. *We* are playing this game, so we make the choices. I want that spirit to be free. I want to hear it say '*A word once given must be honored*' and know it's going to save those children." Jon took a huge gulp of the Coke after this impassioned speech. Barion raised his own bottle and they clinked.

"Amen to that. Let's free the Whispering Hillock." They started punching their gaming keyboards, getting the trapped spirit his bones and the raven feathers and the swift steed before piercing his heart so that his blood would flow for him to live again. When the freed spirit departed, both Barion and Jon whooped.

They played a bit longer then watched the sweet ending on YouTube with Ciri becoming a Witcher and Geralt settling down with Triss. The snacks were all gone by then and a quick glance at the clock on his PC told Jon it was already past ten in the evening. Time had flown in Barion's company, and Jon didn't want it to end just yet.

"Are you hungry?"

Barion got up from his armchair and stretched, his joints popping loudly. "I could eat." He rubbed his belly. "No sugar crap, though. Something substantial. How about pizza?"

Jon got up as well, already looking for his cell. "I can order. What do you like?"

"I'll take a meat lover's pizza, one with mushrooms and egg, a mixed salad, extra garlic bread and a tiramisu for dessert. No, scratch that, they never get it right. Just order the main dishes and I'll make a short trip later to get us the real deal when it comes to Italian sweets."

"Can't wait." Jon dialed the pizza delivery service of Beaconville, giving them Barion's impressive order and adding a Pizza Margarita for himself, as well as a helping of *bruschetta*. Only twenty minutes later, the bell Sammy had installed for Jon's cellar apartment rang. It was Milo, the young man who worked for Sammy in his bookstore. Jon looked at him in surprise.

"Milo, I thought you'd stopped working for the delivery service?"

Milo held out the food and avoided looking at Jon's face. "I need some extra cash," he murmured. Since the young man clearly didn't want to talk about it, Jon refrained from prying further but made a mental note to talk to Sammy first thing tomorrow. The reason his friend had given Milo the job at the bookstore was so that he could concentrate on his studies while earning more money than he did with the delivery. He put the boxes with the food down to get his wallet, but Barion beat him to it, forcing several bills into Milo's hand, with a gruff, "Keep the change."

Milo glanced at the money, then shook his head. "I can't. It's too much."

It probably was, and the boy was much too honest for his own good. Barion held his hands up, his jaw jutting out stubbornly. He looked remarkably like his brother when Dre had set his mind on something. "You keep it. That's my last word."

There was just enough of a demon growl in Barion's voice to have Milo backing away.

"Okay. Thank you." He turned around and almost fled to the stairs leading out of the cellar. Jon smiled at Barion.

"That was very nice of you," Jon said to Barion while he went to the kitchenette to get cutlery.

Barion just shrugged. "Sammy has taken that boy under his wing, which means Dre has too, and that means I'm responsible for him as well. We need to tell Sammy about this."

"I know. I was planning to do it tomorrow."

"Tell me if you need help."

"Thank you, will do." Jon handed Barion a knife and a fork, taking his own tools with him. "Let's watch *The Big Bang Theory* while eating. We could go for the episode with the battle ostrich."

"Great idea." Barion gathered the boxes in his arms before he followed Jon back to the gaming paradise, this time into the corner where Jon had hung his flatscreen on the wall. After a short search, he found the right season and episode and they ate in peace while Jim Parsons hyperventilated into a brown paper bag.

Two episodes later all the food was gone. Jon was sprawled on his comfortable couch, sunken so deep into the upholstery that he wasn't sure if he hadn't already started becoming a part of it. Barion wasn't faring any better, his huge, muscular form half-eaten by the quilt Mavis and Maribel had gifted Jon as consolation after the embarrassing incident with the forgotten brain. The old saying was true. There was rarely something bad that didn't bring something good as well.

"I'm not sure I have the energy to get us dessert." Barion groaned, licking the last crumbs from his lips. Jon stared in fascination.

"I'm not sure I have the energy to eat anything else. I feel like a stuffed turkey. Or I guess, how I think a stuffed turkey must feel, if they could still feel, but they can't, because they're dead—and please stop me rambling. It's the food coma."

Barion chuckled, pulling the quilt farther up his bulky body. "Tell you what. Let's watch one more episode. I suggest the one where Penny gives Sheldon the Christmas present. I love that one. If we still feel too full afterward, we call it a day and I promise to bring those desserts next time we meet. How does that sound?"

"You're a genius. So full of great ideas." Jon hesitated. He usually wasn't that forward, but with Barion, he felt so relaxed, as if he couldn't say anything wrong, couldn't stumble into any of the many traps social interactions posed. "Actually, I wanted to ask if you'd like to come back the day after tomorrow and perhaps do a video with me? I've got this new game called *Eden's Doom,* and they want me to review it. It's a multiplayer game and it would be more fun testing it together."

Barion stared at Jon with his mouth hanging open. It took him quite some time to answer and Jon was starting to feel nervous. "You want me to play with you on an unreleased game and film it for your channel?"

"Uh, yes. Only if you want to, though. We can just play without filming it."

"You would want me in one of your videos?" Barion's voice was full of awe. "That's so cool. Of course I want to!"

"Then it's a deal?" Jon felt a happy giggle forcing its way up in his throat. He suppressed it relentlessly because he didn't want to come across as an absolute idiot.

"More than a deal! When do you want me to come?"

"Uhm, it doesn't matter, whenever it's convenient for you. I don't need to sleep much, and I'm usually up around five."

"Tell you what... I'll come at seven and bring breakfast. Anything you don't like?" Barion was glowing now.

"I'm good with everything, though nothing too hearty early in the morning."

"Got it, lay off the Haggis and *Blutwurst*. Ah, found it." Barion had been looking for the Christmas episode while they talked. Now he pressed play and Jon sank back into the comforting softness of his couch. This, he could get used to.

Chapter Four

Barion was pacing in his living room, thinking so hard that steam was literally curling out of his ears. Tomorrow he would be playing *Eden's Doom* with Jon, and he had yet to find a suitable gamer name for himself. Jon was setting the bar pretty high with PLM, which reminded Barion that he had to ask what it stood for. So far there were a lot of crazy suggestions out there, from it being the initials of Jon's first loves, either in the flesh or gaming characters — people were hazy about that — to some strange code making sense only to people who spent way too much time researching conspiracy theories, all of which Barion dismissed after having spent an entire afternoon and evening with the zombie. He wasn't sure what he wanted his own gamer name to be. There were so many possibilities. For a moment he toyed with the idea to use a demonic name, just for fun, but then he remembered what the 'bit of fun' Corriwyn had wanted to have had meant for demonkind and decided to not go that route, which only left about a million other possibilities.

The name had to be cool, and mysterious, and a bit of fun, perhaps an allusion to something he liked. *Hmm, how can I make a clever reference to* Khachapuri? Barion was so engrossed in the name finding that he almost didn't register the tear in time and space close to the door to the hall, announcing a visitor. Since he had his home warded against unwanted guests, especially of the demonic variety, he was sure it was somebody he'd at least tolerate seeing. He hadn't expected that somebody to be his father, because the old man seemed to be busy all the time, what with being the king of all demons. To Alerion's credit, Barion had to say he made more time for his sons now that Dre had found his mate.

"Son, it's so good to see you!" Alerion hugged Barion.

"It's good to see you, too, Dad. To what do I owe the pleasure?"

"Can't a man just visit his youngest son?" Alerion was leaning back from the hug without letting Barion go, trying for innocent and failing completely. Not that any demon was able to pull off 'innocent' at all. This notion was so contrary to the inherent nature of demons that it was like mixing mousse au chocolat with pickles. No sane person would ever try to do so — well, unless they were pregnant, or so he'd been told. But the normal population? Not even when hell froze over, which wasn't as impossible as people thought, as hell dimensions went through a steady cycle of hot and cold, on a scale of eons, which made it kind of hard to track, plus they were completely uninhabitable, killing anything alive within seconds of arrival. They were the most hostile dimensions Barion had ever come across. Demons could exist everywhere, even though they were, technically, alive, so the hell rule didn't apply to them. It still didn't make hell dimensions any more tempting or inviting. So no, he wasn't buying it.

"A man can, but the king of all demons cannot. What are you up to?"

Alerion sighed dramatically while he stepped back, letting go of Barion's shoulders, to sit down on his couch. "I'm here to invite you to a nice evening with Swiss cheese fondue in Lausanne."

"And?" Barion knew his father too well to fall for his act.

"And Dre and Sammy might be coming, too, wanting to talk to you about your play date with Jon?" Alerion had the grace to look sheepish.

Barion sighed inwardly. Of course his nosy brother-in-law had gotten wind of their get together.

"Why are you doing everything Sammy wants?" he asked his father accusingly. Alerion lifted his hands in defense.

"That's not true. I love all my children equally and try to be fair to all of you." He had the gall to look offended.

"Stop it, Dad. We all know Sammy is your favorite."

"Well, he is a lot cuter than the lot of you. You've got to admit that. I mean, just look at his beautiful bi-colored eyes and the way he bites his lips when he finds a new book he likes. And he hasn't set anything on fire yet or tried to kill me with his cooking. Actually, his cooking is delicious."

"I get it. Sammy is perfect." Barion huffed in mock-annoyance. He liked Sammy as well. "But he can't set anything on fire because he doesn't have the power, and I didn't try to kill you. I wanted to make you happy."

"I'm not sure about happy, but it was definitely memorable." Alerion patted Barion's shoulder. "Now get ready. We're already a little late."

"I haven't said I'd come."

Alerion just lifted a brow. Barion huffed. "Fine. Are you doing the honors?"

"As if I'd let you drive." Alerion snorted before he lifted his hand, ripping thin air again. Barion stepped closer to his father so they could enter the portal together.

"I don't think this is technically driving, and I've been doing this for centuries. Just saying."

"It's the equivalent of driving and I don't care how long you've been doing this. I've still got more experience."

They stepped into a side street close to Parc de Milan, which was still quite busy at eight p.m. The glamour demons carried with them protected them from being discovered, making them look like two impressively tall men in dark clothing, but still human men, not eight foot plus demons. People avoided them nevertheless, their survival instincts still strong enough to recognize apex predators in their midst, despite the sense-numbing lives they lived. From Rue Voltaire they went left into Rue Jean-Louis-de-Bons where the restaurant they would be visiting was located. It was one of Barion's family's favorite restaurants, much like the one Zenobia ran in Rome. This one, the *Faucon*, was owned by a family of falcons who had been living in Lausanne almost as long as the city had existed.

When they entered, Ottilie, the daughter of the matriarch, greeted them with a broad smile. "*Bienvenue*, Alerion, Barion. It's a pleasure to see you. Dresalantion and his *bien-aimé* are waiting in the private room."

Alerion took Ottilie's hand and kissed it. "*Enchanté, ma chéré*. It's our pleasure to be here tonight."

Barion rolled his eyes behind his father's back. *The old sweet-talker*. Ottilie giggled happily, grabbing Alerion's hand and leading them through a hall past the main eating room toward the private rooms where the most revered and financially potent guests were seated. The whole restaurant was decked in warm earth tones with golden highlights, giving it a cozy, yet elegant feeling. The door to their usual room was open and Barion saw Dre and Sammy already sitting at the table on the thickly upholstered chairs in dark brown with golden seams. Sammy was talking animatedly to Brice, Ottilie's brother, the human's hands waving wildly through the air while his eyes gleamed happily. Brice had that glazed-over look people often got around Sammy while Dre was hanging onto his mate's every word with an indulgent, proud smile on his lips.

"Oh, I see my son-in-law is already making friends," Alerion commented while stepping inside the room.

"He's such a wonderful, gentle person. Dresalantion is lucky to have him," Ottilie said, while closing the door behind Barion.

Sammy had now spied them and squealed happily. "Dad, Barion! You're here!" He got up from his chair to hug Alerion, who closed his powerful arms around the fragile human with the utmost care.

"Sammy, it's so good to see you."

"Did you know that Lausanne has existed since before the second century AD and was once a Roman military camp, built on a former Celtic settlement, so it's probably even older. They called it Lousanna, and later it was known as vikanor Lousonnensium but, by 400, it was civitas Lausanna and in 990 it was mentioned as Losanna. And Brice here says his ancestors came here with the Romans and have been living in the city ever since. He's going to give me a tour next spring, when it's warmer and the trees are blossoming."

Sammy looked very happy about everything he had learned, which was his natural state when he gained new wisdom to add to his vast pool of knowledge. Alerion smiled down on Sammy's wild curls, while sending Brice a grateful nod, who accepted it with a slight bow. "You couldn't wish for a better guide. Brice is very knowledgeable about the history of Lausanne and can show you places not even most natives are acquainted with."

"*Oui*," Brice said. "You're going to love it, *bien-aimé* of Dresalantion."

"You should really call me Sammy, Brice."

"As you wish, Sammy." Brice bowed again before he pulled out a chair for Alerion.

"It's such a shame we know so little about the time when it was a Celtic settlement." Sammy sighed, snuggling into Dre's side. Both Dre and Alerion, who had taken his seat, were shooting Barion a look. For a moment he resisted, knowing he would condemn himself to a lifetime of slavery to Sammy, but when he saw how devastated his brother-in-law was over knowledge lost to time, he relented. While he sat down on the chair Brice had pulled out for him, he addressed Sammy. "I could show you."

Sammy stared at him. "Show me what?"

"The Celtic settlement…if you want."

Sammy's eyes grew huge. "Really? How?"

"You remember I told you how every member of the royal family has a special talent, *mo grah thu*?" Dre took Sammy's hand and started stroking it.

"Yes. You also said nobody can know because it's a secret of the demon in question, and I respect that."

"I know, Sammy. We know." Dre looked at his father and Barion. Ottilie and Brice had left the room, ever the gracious hosts leaving the demons to their private conversation. "And Barion has decided to let you know his talent."

Sammy's lips formed an O of utter surprise and delight. He got up from his chair, and before he knew what was happening, Barion felt himself hugged to within an inch of his life. "This is such an honor, Barion! Thank you, thank you, thank you. But I would love you anyway, if you told me or not. You know that, don't you? You're my brother."

Sammy was so genuinely concerned that any resentment Barion might have felt about having been gently urged to reveal his talent dispersed. Sammy deserved all the happiness in the world.

"I know, Sammy. And it's fine, really. It's nothing terrible anyway. Almost a little embarrassing, considering my lack of interest in history."

"What is it? What can you do?" Sammy was now almost vibrating out of his skin.

Barion grinned. "I can show you any event in history you want to see...like a documentary film."

For a moment, Sammy didn't say anything and Barion was afraid he may have broken the human. They were a delicate bunch after all. Then Sammy squealed.

"Dre, did you hear that? Oh, you don't need to hear it. You already knew. I'm almost angry at you for not telling me, but I get the thing with the secret. Now, is there a chance of Barion moving in with us? There's so much we need to see, and just imagine, Dre, we could take Barion with us so we can watch history take place where it took place? That didn't come out right, did it?"

"It's fine, *mo grah thu*. But, Sammy, I don't think Barion wants to become our personal history showman. Perhaps we could convince him to come with us once a month? Besides, isn't it also interesting to *imagine* how things had been? To weave our tales?"

"You're right, Dre. Totally right. I just got carried away. That's an awesome talent, Barion. Not embarrassing at all. On the contrary, I'm tempted to say it's better than being chaos personified." Sammy winked at Dre, taking any and all sharpness out of his words. Dre mock gasped.

"I'm horrified, *mo grah thu*...horrified."

Alerion was laughing so hard that tears were streaming down his face.

Barion decided to put an end to the discussion. He was getting hungry and Ottilie and Brice wouldn't come back before they were called. "Yes, I'm willing to show you what went on here in Lausanne before it became a Roman settlement. No, we're not doing it right now because we're all hungry, and yes, I could be persuaded to go with you on history trips once a month with the right incentive but no, re-organizing my library is *not* an incentive."

Sammy pouted. "I'm working hard on it, you know?"

Now Barion felt like an asshole. "I'm sorry, Sammy. I know you mean well. I just have problems getting accustomed to your way of organizing everything."

"Oh, that's no problem. Next time, you can help me, and I can explain to you what I'm doing and why."

Dre and Alerion were wiping tears of joy from their eyes while Barion tried to wriggle out of that one. Of course they wouldn't help him. "Uhm, that's very nice of you, Sammy. We'll see. Now how about we call Ottilie and Brice back? Have you ever had Swiss cheese fondue?"

The mention of food was enough to distract Sammy for the moment and Barion was able to relax a little, though it didn't last long. Once Brice had brought the baskets with delicious bread and the steaming pot of melted cheeses—Gruyere, Emmental and Gouda, the classic mixture for fondue—they started eating, and with the dunking of the bread into the cheese came the questions.

"So, you and Jon spent the day together?" Sammy was even worse at being subtle than Dre and Alerion, which was saying a lot. Barion decided not to be cowed. Sammy was just looking out for his friend and tenant, and Barion hadn't done anything wrong.

"Yes, we played *The Witcher III: Wild Hunt* for a bit. We thought together we might be brave enough to betray the Whispering Hillock, but we like the horse too much."

Dre huffed around a mouthful of cheese and bread. "I'm not even going to pretend I understood the second sentence at all."

"I can break it down for you. Jon and I play game. Big game. Many choices. We not make one choice."

"I hate you." Dre dunked another bread into the cheese.

"You love me."

"You're family. Love is built in." Sammy was trying to get another bread on the fork-like tool they used to get the cheese out of the pot. Alerion absently took it from him and expertly stabbed the bread. "Thank you, Dad. Now back to Jon. What are your intentions with him? Because he's a good guy and my friend and I want him to be happy."

"I can assure you, Sammy, my intentions are pure. I like Jon, he's fun to hang out with, he loves video games, the same as I do, and we had a blast playing last time. I'm looking forward to tomorrow."

"You're meeting again?" There was a gleam in Sammy's eyes and Barion knew he had to act fast if he didn't want an unwanted audience during his gaming day with Jon.

"Yes, and we're going to play video games the entire time, which will bore you to death, but I promise I'll check in with you before I leave."

"And when you arrive." Sammy sounded a lot like a worried parent.

"And when I arrive." Barion sighed. "I promised Jon breakfast. Can I bring you something as well?" It was always a good idea to have food handy to placate the beast.

"Dre? I know Jon loves crêpes, and I could do with one as well…or two. Make that three. One hearty, two sweet. From the café in Paris you recommended."

"Yeah, sounds good. I'll take six, half hearty, half sweet. Thank you, brother." Dre smiled broadly at him, showing a hint of fang, which would have been more impressive if there hadn't been a bit of cheese dangling from it.

Barion sighed. "Will do. Now can we please talk about something else?"

Chapter Five

Jon was pacing again. This seemed to be his default when it came to waiting for Barion. He was a bit unsure if twice was enough to qualify as a repetitive behavioral pattern, but since he usually didn't even do once with other people, twice was a two hundred percent increase, which had to be good. Unless you counted pacing as a nervous habit then increasing it wasn't good at all and, oh gods, he'd need a shrink, one who made house calls—and where would he find one of those without Sammy and Dre and the others getting wind of it, not to mention Grann, who would tell him to come home immediately. *Why is it so difficult to get a life?* The irony in that question had him chuckling.

The sound of steps on the stairs pulled him out of this train of thought that was rapidly heading toward a very dark tunnel. Barion's voice was clear on the other side of his door.

"I told you, Sammy, it's fine. I can carry breakfast for Jon and me. It's not that heavy. Plus, I could have just taken the short cut into his apartment."

"No, really, Barion, I want to help." Sammy had this stubborn tone Jon knew all too well. His friend and landlord was in meddling mode, born out of true worry for Jon, which was the only reason Jon was willing to accept it. Barion must have thought along similar lines, because despite his own tone carrying a hint of exasperation, he was patient with Sammy.

"Sammy, Jon and I are fine. I'm not going to kill him or leave him stranded in some weird-ass dimension. We're just playing a video game!"

"You'd leave him in another dimension?" Of course Sammy would latch onto that. Jon grinned, wondering how Barion would weasel out of it.

"Never! That's what I said. He's perfectly safe with me."

"But you could." Sammy was more stubborn than a mule in front of a dark patch on the ground. Barion's sigh was long-suffering.

"Dre, could you please tell your mate I would never, in all my life, leave Jon in another dimension."

So Dre is there as well. Not really a surprise.

"Sammy, Barion would never, in all his life, leave Jon in another dimension. Time seems to be still on the table, though."

"Dre, you asshole!"

Jon heard heavy thumping, indicating two demons play-wrestling. It was enough for Jon to make him fear for his door and the hall. He stepped forward and opened it.

"Good morning, Barion, Sammy, Dre. How are you?"

Sammy smiled happily at him, while Barion looked up from where he was trying to strangle Dre from two steps below him, which made quite the picture.

"Good morning, Jon. Barion was just assuring me he would never leave you stranded in a strange dimension, but as my highly intelligent mate has pointed out, we haven't yet established if he wouldn't leave you somewhere else in time." Sammy cocked his head. "Sounds a bit like *Dr. Who*, if you ask me."

Jon felt his lips turn into an even wider grin, the way Sammy's eyes were sparkling telling him he was mostly yanking Barion's chain. The friendly human could be quite mischievous when he wanted to be.

"Yep, sounds definitely like *Dr. Who*. And you can rest assured that we're only playing a game today — no going out into the world, not to mention other dimensions."

"You don't know what you're missing." Sammy clapped his hands. "We're leaving you two alone. Have fun."

"But things were getting good," Dre whined.

"Yeah, I was close to finally getting rid of you," Barion spat back.

"In your dreams!"

The temperature in the hall was suddenly rising and Jon didn't know what to do. He wasn't a fan of violence, at least not when it happened in real life. And though he had gotten used to the casual fights in the book club — shifters and vampires were a volatile bunch, especially when they were of differing opinions on the matter of female representation in the *Dragonriders of Pern* novels by Anne McCaffrey — two demons getting serious was way out of his league.

Luckily for him, Sammy had no qualms about getting between the two brothers, whose intricate tattoos had started to glow so brightly that Jon could see them through the clothing they wore which was…yummy, if he were completely honest with himself. *Very yummy indeed.* The light was just strong enough to emphasize Barion's perfectly muscled body underneath the sweatshirt and designer jeans, both of which didn't leave much to the imagination to begin with. Seeing all those cloth-encased muscles highlighted like a painting by an old master reminded Jon of his sex drive, the very thing he had thought he'd lost forever.

He shook his head. Thinking of Barion and sexiness and muscles and sex was wrong. *So wrong.* Even though he couldn't seem to remember why. He heard a huff. Ah, yes, because Barion and Dre were *this* close to a full-on fight, and Jon had to protect Sammy or the members of the book club would kill him.

"Dre, Barion, stop it or I'm telling Dad." The words were like a bucket of ice-water. The demon brothers turned to Sammy.

"You wouldn't!" Dre's eyes were wide with disbelief.

"Watch me. You two love each other, and you know it. So why do you always have to escalate things?"

"That's what demons do, *mo grah thu.*"

"Yes, Sammy, we've been like this since we were small."

Sammy crossed his arms in front of his chest. "Well, I don't like it, so stop." The devious little devil even managed to let his bottom lip tremble the tiniest bit. Jon had to applaud Sammy's talent for acting.

"It's okay, *mo grah thu*. We were just joking. Everything's fine, isn't it, Barion?"

"Of course, brother. We simply got carried away, Sammy."

Both demons almost fell over themselves to placate Sammy. After a few more reassurances, Sammy and Dre went back upstairs and Barion entered Jon's apartment.

"Sorry about that. Sammy insisted on coming down with me and Dre always manages to rile me up."

"It's fine. I know everything about annoying family." Jon thought about all of his relatives and shuddered. Intent on leaving this topic behind, he looked at the box Barion had picked up from the ground after his attempt to get rid of his brother. "Please tell me this is breakfast. I think I'm starving."

"It is breakfast. Crêpes from a quaint little café in Paris, the best you'll ever taste." Barion opened the box and the smells wafting up made Jon an instant believer.

"What do we have?"

"This here is with Parma ham and *Le Beaufort Chalet d'Alpage*, a very expensive cheese worth every penny it costs. I think you'll like how the saltiness of the Parma ham harmonizes with the complex taste of the matured cheese. Then we have one with *Fromage fraise* made from goat's milk paired with spinach and garlic and the last variety is Roquefort with figs, walnuts and Leatherwood Honey. As dessert I have brought crêpes with a filling of strawberries and cream, applesauce with sugar and cinnamon and a hint of cider, as well as the classic nougat cream made with seventy percent hazelnuts."

"In other words, not death by sugar overload as would be the case with Nutella." Jon found Barion's enthusiasm about food endearing.

"No, no Nutella." Barion shuddered. "Once you've tasted what nougat cream can be like, Nutella becomes nothing but a bad memory."

"I'll take your word for it. Let's get the goods over to the gaming room and I'll get us plates and cutlery. The game is ready and the camera focused, so we can start right away."

"Great. I can't wait."

Jon went to the kitchen in a hurry because he didn't want the crêpes to get cold. Once they were seated, Barion put the ones with the Parma ham on their plates and Jon couldn't suppress a moan when he got the first taste of salty crunchiness mixed with soft dough and the almost biting flavor of the cheese. Barion sure knew what was good. They ate the first crêpes in deferential silence, showing the excellent food the respect it deserved. Before they started with the spinach crêpes, Jon asked Barion, "How should I introduce you, by the way? Do you have a gamer name you'd like to use?"

Barion sighed. "I've been thinking forever about it, trying to come up with clever puns or names but it seems I'm not that creative. So it's going to be my WoW name, Big B."

Jon bit back a chuckle. "Big B isn't so bad. It certainly fits."

"Yeah, there's that. Which reminds me, what does PLM stand for? Did you know there's tons of theories out there about your name? Some of them quite disturbing, I might add."

Jon laughed. "I know. People can get quite inventive." He turned serious. "Nobody but me knows what the letters stand for. Well, Grann could probably guess it if she knew about the name."

"You don't have to tell me, Jon. Keeping secrets is fine. That just makes me more interested in getting to know you better." Barion winked.

If Jon hadn't known better, he would have thought Barion was flirting with him, but that couldn't be the case because he knew from Sammy that Barion was looking for his mate, not some quick fling or short affair. Jon didn't even know if he wanted to have one of those. Technically, he was looking for something serious as well, though he doubted zombies had fated mates. At least he'd never heard of it, and he had been too chicken to ask Grann, in case she decided to take matters in her own hands and find him someone. Her meddling was bad enough as it was. Despite all those logical thoughts running through his mind, Jon felt the urge to tell Barion this secret he kept more out of habit than anything else.

"You can't tell anybody."

Barion put one hand over where Jon thought the heart was located with demons and held the other one out to him, his pinkie finger extended. "Pinkie swear."

That was so ridiculous that Jon had to chuckle. Then he hooked his own pinkie with Barion's to seal the deal. The sudden heat surging through him from the point where their skin met reminded him of how cold he always was, but for the first time, it didn't bother him. Perhaps because his thoughts were occupied otherwise. "Pinkie swear."

They shook and after unhooking their fingers, Jon took a deep breath. "PLM stands for Papa Legba's Miracle. It's what Grann called me after I was resurrected. She says Papa Legba works in mysterious ways and him waking me along with her had to have some secret reason. We don't know what that reason is yet, though."

"Well, I have to admit that's kind of anticlimactic." Barion pretended to be disappointed. Jon wasn't fooled though, because the laughter in his eyes gave the demon away. "You sure it's not some secret code for the end of the world or something?"

"I'd say me coming back from the dead is spectacular enough. I could be wrong, though."

"It is pretty impressive, I guess." Barion shrugged.

"You *guess*?"

"Demons are immortal...and more or less indestructible. So yes, I guess because I don't have a frame of reference there."

For a moment Jon was speechless. "Now I understand what Maribel meant when she said demons are different."

Barion shrugged. "We are. Doesn't mean we don't want the same things as everybody else."

"Like a mate." Jon had picked up on the longing in Barion's voice.

"A mate, friends, love, companionship. I know demons aren't necessarily associated with those things."

"It's okay, Barion. Most people think all zombies want is a brain to eat."

"Don't you?" Barion winked.

"Only once a week. And I have to say I'm not particularly fond of human brains. I prefer calf or pig."

"What is so bad about human brains? I'm asking purely out of interest, of course."

"Of course. Well, first there's the whole 'where to get it without murdering somebody and drawing a crowd with guns and pitchforks' issue. Plus, for reasons unbeknownst to me, people don't like it when the brains of their deceased are taken out, even though the Egyptians have done it for thousands of years. And lastly, human brain tastes strange. Grann says it has to do with the spirit that has lived inside the body, but frankly, I think it has more to do with what humans eat these days."

"So no human brains for you."

Jon shuddered. "Not if I can help it." He used his fork to get one of the crêpes with the strawberries and cream out. It was delicious, the ripe strawberries so sweet that it was almost too much. *Almost.* "So good. Thank you for bringing these."

"It was my pleasure. And thank you for letting me play with you. That's an honor."

"About that, is it okay for you if we do it live? People dig that and it would be a nice surprise for my subscribers."

"If you think I can do it. It's my first time."

"You can't do anything wrong. We're commenting on the game as we play it. That's all."

Barion didn't look entirely convinced, so Jon decided to jump right in. He put his plate away, got comfortable with his Aukey KM G6 gaming keyboard, and started the game when he saw Barion was ready to go. "Okay, we're live in three, two, one, go." He activated the cameras and the microphones, keeping their faces well hidden while allowing glimpses into their surroundings—nothing much, just enough to keep people wondering who and where they were— and, of course, fully highlighting the screens.

"Welcome, friends and fellow gamers, this is PLM with another live stream and today I have a guest, Big B, who will help me play the first levels of *Eden's Doom*, a game you've surely all heard about. It'll release in two weeks and expectations in the community are high. Let's see what we've got."

Jon glanced at the live stream of comments in the lower right side of his screen, seeing that people were already getting into gear, asking who Big B was and telling each other to post about the stream. Clicks were increasing by the second, the number of viewers leaping from only twenty to over four hundred within minutes, then turning into a steady rise Jon knew could go up to five-digit numbers depending on how quickly word got around. It was a great start.

"Upon starting the game, I can already say I like the soundtrack. The opening music is majestic and promising, tickling interest in what's to come. Big B, your thoughts?"

For a moment Barion seemed to be frozen. Then he took a deep breath and started talking. "Hi, everybody, this is Big B. I'm so happy to be here today and I'm asking you to bear with me as I find my footing. Sitting next to PLM is such an honor!"

I'm jealous.

You're right, but I'm sure you'll rock.

Start playing and we'll see.

Welcome, Big B.

The comments were mostly positive and more fixated on the game than on Barion, which was good. The demon relaxed even more and started talking about the set-up of the game.

"Like PLM said, I dig the music. It's captivating and a promising start. The menu looks easy enough to handle, everything's pretty clear-cut, no complicated loops to jump through."

"First, we have to choose our character." Jon clicked the icon—a flaming door—to get into the Hall of Angels and Demons. "Nice graphics, not as realistic as some others we've seen lately but decent."

"Yeah. Let's see who we're going to play. Any suggestions?" Barion was already including the viewers like a pro. The clicks were now at twenty-thousand and still increasing. Not bad for a morning, though it wasn't morning everywhere his subscribers sat in front of their PCs.

Play an angel.

Yeah, the big one with the black wings.

No, take the one with the broadsword.

I think they should be demons for the first round.

How about the green one that looks a bit like the Hulk?

The comments were getting heated, and Jon knew he had to put an end to it quickly if he didn't want things to escalate. Gamers could be an excitable bunch. And the way Barion was eyeing the demonic characters, Jon knew they had to choose angels for the first round.

"I'll take the angel with the black wings, Muorte. Death, I guess. Big B?"

"The one with the broadsword looks good. Michaele. One thing's for sure... They weren't overly inventive when it comes to names. Though that's perhaps good as well because that way there's already associations to help the players get into the characters."

True.

I like it.

I think it's boring.

Is borrowing from a certain religion-culture offensive?

No, I don't think so.

Could be.

On and on it went while Barion and Jon got the basic weapons and armor for their characters.

"I'm not sure I like that there's no choosing what you want." Jon frowned at the screen where his angel was picking up a scythe. "Usually the player has more freedom in endowing their character. Here we are limited to what the game provides."

"Could be interesting, though. We have to deal with what we got." Barion let his angel put on the huge armor he was supposed to wear.

"Let's see. I'm not convinced."

The first level had them patrolling the walls protecting Eden, with some smaller fights against low-level demons. It was meant to give the players a chance to get used to their characters and the handling of the game, the reaction time of the console and the graphics. Jon praised it as a good idea while Barion thought it was a wasted level. Comments were divided, some agreeing with Jon, others with Barion.

They played for ninety minutes, going through three levels, none of which was overwhelming. Viewer numbers topped out at thirty-six thousand, which meant a nice bonus for Jon, so he was satisfied. He stopped the game.

"Thank you for tuning in today. If you're interested in another live stream of *Eden's Doom*, please let me know and we'll set up another date. Have a wonderful day and happy gaming, your PLM and Big B!"

"Bye everybody and thank you for bearing with me."

No problem at all.

You were great.

So funny.

We need another live stream!

The comments were exploding while Jon shut the microphones and the cameras off. When everything was private again, he grinned at Barion.

"You were great! This was so much fun! Thank you."

The demon grinned so broadly that Jon got full view of his impressive fangs. "I have to thank you. I barely realized time was going by. And I'd love to do another stream with you."

"We just have to set up a date. Let's see what the comments say, then we can talk about when would be a good time." Jon got up from his lounge chair and stretched. Barion followed suit, his back cracking like machine gun fire.

"Ah, I need a break. What do you do when you're not gaming?"

Jon thought about it. "Reading. Or just sitting around, doing nothing."

Barion shook his head. "That won't do. I need to move. Have you ever been to the Carpathians?"

"No?"

"No, as in you don't know where the Carpathians are, or no, as in you have no desire to go there?"

"No, as in I don't know where you're going with that question." Jon stared at Barion.

"Ah, I see. Well, I'm inviting you to my cozy little home. I mean, it's only fair. I've been at your place twice. You have to see mine as well."

"Uhm, that's fine. I'm not keeping tabs." Jon wasn't sure what to think. He was excited by the invitation — excited and scared to death. He didn't go out. He didn't visit other people's homes. He stayed there, in his cellar, where it was safe and quiet and just him and his computers. Barion didn't seem to care, because he grabbed Jon's hand, apparently having forgotten about not touching him, and Jon found he didn't mind. Perhaps it was because Barion ran so hot that there was no mistaking him for a human. A human with Barion's skin temperature would have been well on their way to the final slumber and not jumping up and down like a giddy three-year-old on a sugar rush.

"Come on. You'll love it."

"Fine. Show me your home."

Barion lifted the hand not holding on to Jon and extended one of his claws — his very long claws. Jon felt his eyes widen. Barion saw it and looked a bit sheepish. "Sorry. I need the full length to open time and space. I know they look frightening."

"That's not it." Jon shook his head. "I've just never seen claws that long. I mean Emilia's are quite impressive, her being an ancient vampire and all, but yours are just...wow."

Barion seemed to grow in front of Jon's eyes. "Wait till you see my wings!"

"You don't mean in here?"

"No. Too cramped. I wouldn't be able to fully extend them. I'll show you when we're at my place."

Barion lifted his hand again, the claw making a clean slice in thin air before dragging Jon through without much fanfare. After a moment of intense disorientation, Jon found himself in a living room with a bright orange leather couch and a huge flatscreen on the wall.

Chapter Six

Jon felt Barion watching him closely as they stood in the middle of his living room. Here in the Carpathians, it was already late afternoon, and the sun was getting ready to set behind the mountains, painting them in a gorgeous violet hue. Now that he had Jon in his home, he suddenly seemed unsure what to do, which Jon could relate to. He, too, wasn't sure what he was even doing here.

"Do you want a tour?"

Jon shook his head like a kitten that had gotten wet, his dark strands shivering around his face. "Yeah. Yeah. After you've explained to me what exactly is *little* about your home."

Barion grinned. "Come on. It's not that big."

"Not that big? Your living room is bigger than my entire apartment. Why did you even agree to go there a second time when you have this at your disposal?"

"Because you aren't here. Weren't here." The words came out so fast that Jon had problems understanding them. When he did, he must have looked at Barion funny, because the demon started babbling nervously. "I mean, we wanted to play together, and I think your apartment is really cool, especially your gaming set-up. Mine isn't half as good, and you've got all the equipment and…"

Jon lifted his hand, trying and failing to suppress a grin. "I get it, Barion. I guess I'm just as smitten with your home as you apparently were with mine."

"So, we do the tour?"

"I *so* want a tour. And don't forget to show me the library, aka 'halls of chaos', if Sammy is to be believed."

"They're chaos now." Barion made a sweeping gesture with his right hand. "Please follow me." He first brought Jon to his dining room where a stag head encrusted with jewels hung on the wall. It was gorgeous and a bit creepy, though in a good way. Jon stared at it with big eyes.

"Are those real?"

"Yes. For a few centuries, I thought collecting gemstones was fun, and so I had a broad range to choose from."

"It's absolutely beautiful. I like the Damien Hirst vibe, and you definitely gave it your own spin. Aren't you afraid of thieves?"

"Uhm, in case you haven't noticed, Jon, I'm a demon. Any human or paranormal dumb enough to enter this place and try to steal something deserves what they have coming to them."

"Which would be?" Jon lifted one of his brows, wanting to know, while not wanting to know what a demon would do to somebody who trespassed on their property. His imagination did provide some detailed ideas, which he wished he could un-think.

"I'm not at liberty to say, but rest assured, they would never ever think about stealing anything again." Barion waggled his eyebrows, which had Jon giggling.

"Okay, no human or paranormal thieves for you. What about other demons?"

"A possibility, which is the reason this place is heavily warded, though any demon reckless enough to steal from one of the princes would find themselves in one of the dungeon dimensions."

"They do exist?" Jon was honestly interested, and Barion seemed happy to be able to talk to somebody about these things without the person freaking out on him.

"There's plenty, though not all of them are prisons. Some are actually quite nice, if you like rocks and the colors red and brown." He winked to show he was joking. "In fact, a lot of the dungeon dimensions are colorful places where life is going crazy with experiments, which makes them a bit unsafe for non-demons. If a bee the size of a horse decides to attack, things can get dicey, though being bitten by a mouse with more poison than an Inland Taipan from Earth surely isn't much better." Barion looked totally serious while saying this.

"You're making fun of me." Jon grinned.

"A bit. Tell you what... I'm going to take you to one of the dungeon dimensions this weekend. How does that sound?"

Jon mulled that over. His initial reaction was a *hell, yes, why don't we go now?* while his brain tried to remind him that he wasn't the adventurous type and what did he think he was doing here anyway? *Building a friendship?* another inner voice suggested, leaving Jon torn.

"I'm sure you know I usually don't go out much. I'm not good with people and it's always disappointing," he finally said, and even in his own ears it sounded lame.

"There are no people in the dungeon dimensions," Barion replied. *They wouldn't survive long*. He didn't say that out loud, but Jon could read it clearly in his eyes. Strangely enough, the idea of going somewhere so dangerous with Barion was what tipped the scales in favor of this adventure. "I think I'd love to go."

Barion's eyes lit up in joy, which in turn made Jon feel infinitely better about this decision that was so out of character for him.

"Then it's a deal. Come on. You haven't seen my library yet."

Barion led the way into his library, where they were greeted by stacks of books on every available surface while the shelves were mostly empty or only partly filled. Jon stared for a moment before he turned to Barion.

"You're right. Sammy is a menace. I can't believe he lets all those books lie around like that."

"He says he's still in the process of taking stock, whatever that means."

"You mean you don't have a list of them?" Jon knew he probably sounded as horrified as Sammy surely had been when he'd found out about this. Barion simply shrugged, as if it wasn't a big deal.

"When I see a book I like, I bring it here and put it somewhere I think it should be. That's it."

"That's it? You have no clue what you have in here?" Jon was equally parts repelled and fascinated by that idea. In his opinion, not knowing what you had in your library was like not knowing how your WoW account was stocked.

Barion didn't seem to share that sentiment. He scratched his head. "Well, as you can see, there are a lot of them, and I kind of lost track after the first couple of hundred. I like to think of this library as some kind of treasure chest. Every time I come here, I get a surprise."

Jon shook his head. "I understand where the feud between Sammy and you is coming from. I'm seriously torn between wanting to support you in your right to store your books any way you want and the urge to give you a Gibbs slap for being so neglectful."

"Thank you," Barion replied dryly. "I feel so loved."

"Hey, I said I was torn!"

"Too late. I'm officially offended." Barion managed to keep a straight face for about four seconds. When he cracked a grin, Jon smacked him on the arm. The brief skin contact did funny things to his body, things he didn't want to examine too closely, so he turned to leave 'Chaos Central'.

"Let's have dinner and watch some movies?" Barion sounded hopeful and Jon was hungry. All that gaming had taken its toll.

"Wouldn't that be lunch?"

"If we were still in Beaconville, yes. But we're in the Carpathians and it's dinner time."

"Semantics. I could eat, though."

"How about you get comfortable in the living room, and I do a quick tour to Rome to get us pizza?"

"Who could say no to such an offer?" Jon followed Barion into the living room with a huge smile on his face. Pizza sounded perfect.

"You can select a film if you want. Anything you don't like on your pizza?"

"I'm fine with everything."

"Understood. Everything it will be."

Before Jon could react to what he hoped was just a joke, Barion had vanished through another rip in time and space. Knowing he wouldn't take long to return, Jon searched for the remote of the flatscreen to wake it up. Apparently Barion had been watching something and forgotten to switch it off because the screen came to life with the familiar logo of YouTube and a film paused in the middle. Jon's eyes widened when he realized what he was looking at, then he chuckled. It seemed Barion and he had even more in common than just a love for playing video games. Apparently, they both were also suckers for slightly inappropriate love stories within video games as well.

Deciding this was the film he'd want to see if Barion was okay with it, Jon put it back to the beginning, staring at the opening picture where Iron Bull and his Kadan of *Dragon Age: Inquisition* were talking for the first time. The graphics did look a bit clunky, but to be fair, the game had been released in 2014 and programming had evolved greatly since then. The story itself was beautiful and surprisingly romantic, not only for a video game but also for something that was, strictly speaking, interspecies BDSM. It was one of the things Jon loved about the gaming community. Most of them were open-minded and laid back. Jon made himself comfortable on the orange couch and waited for Barion.

Barion grinned when he popped back into his living room. He had taken a little longer due to a detour to France to get some crème brûlée for dessert and hoped Jon didn't mind. The zombie was sitting on the couch, looking utterly comfortable, which in turn made Barion all warm inside. He found it oddly satisfying to provide for Jon.

"Hi, I brought pizza and dessert." He put the four pizza boxes and the container with the crème brûlée on the coffee table. Jon eyed the stack with a certain amount of suspicion.

"Who do you want to feed? An army?"

"I'm better than any army," Barion retorted, waggling his eyebrows wildly. Jon started giggling.

"I do admire your confidence. What have you brought?" He leaned forward to open the box on top. "Oooh, cherry tomatoes, basil and buffalo mozzarella, from the look of things."

"Yes. I love that it's creamier than the one made from cow milk. Also, I like the way cherry tomatoes kind of explode in your mouth with taste and juice." Barion hadn't meant for the words to sound flirty or sexual, but they certainly did. Jon either didn't notice or was very good at hiding his reaction. He simply put the box down to open the next. The other pizzas found his approval as well, one with Parma ham and rucola, one *quattro formaggi* and the last one with artichoke and mushrooms. Barion got the pizza slicer from the kitchen, as well as two plates and two spoons for dessert. After he had cut up all four pizzas and they each had two slices on their plates, he turned to Jon.

"Have you chosen a movie already?"

All of a sudden Jon appeared to be a bit flustered. "Uh, yeah, but only if you're fine with it."

"I'm easy. I watch almost everything."

Jon opened his mouth as if he wanted to say something, then closed it and simply turned the screen on. The moment Barion saw Iron Bull's scarred face, he understood Jon's nervousness, because he felt heat rushing into his cheeks with so much force that he was surprised his scales didn't burn off. "Uhm..." was all he got out.

"I'm sorry." Jon started fumbling with the remote, letting it drop in the process. "It's just that it was on because you had the screen on standby. I do that all the time, you know, because that's how you found out about me being PLM, and really, I love this story, even though the graphics are kind of outdated, but we can totally watch something different."

"It's fine. A bit embarrassing, but fine. I love the story as well, especially the thing with the watchword."

"And when the others walk in on them."

"Yeah. And when Kadan tells Iron Bull he wants to marry him." Barion grinned broadly. He found it both hilarious and sad how a video game showed a healthier relationship between two strong people than many so-called sophisticated stories and films.

"So it's okay to watch this?" Jon still sounded unsure.

"It obviously is. I mean, I had it on, so I can't claim I'm offended or some shit, and you seem to know it as well. No need pretending anything when we're agreeable on the matter." If he were honest, Barion wasn't nearly as sure about watching this together with Jon as he made it sound. The idea stirred feelings in him he wasn't sure what to make of. But he really wanted to make Jon feel comfortable around him, because hanging out with the zombie was a lot more fun than Barion had anticipated.

"Here we go then." Jon picked the remote back up from where it had fallen between two cushions to start the video on YouTube. "And thanks to the kind soul who went through the trouble to put the whole story out there."

"Cheers." Barion lifted his pizza slice in Jon's direction. The video started playing and they enjoyed their meal in a slightly sexually charged silence that took on steam with every appreciative moan over the excellent food. They were done eating shortly after the video came to an end. Barion reached for the remote.

"How about something light for dessert?"

Jon nodded eagerly. "Do you want to stay with the video games or go for a real film instead?"

"Hmm, good question. There are some great videos out there, but how about a comedy for a change? I haven't seen the second *Jumanji* film with The Rock yet."

"Wonderful idea! It's a kind of a game, yet a film, and certainly funny. I loved the first one." Jon was reaching for the bag with the crème brûlée, taking out the two bowls and holding one out to Barion. He took it with a graceful nod, while searching for the film. Once the opening credits rolled, they both leaned back on the couch, their treats in hand, enjoying the movie.

Chapter Seven

When Barion brought Jon home, it was only seven a.m. in Beaconville, which had Jon a bit confused, because in the Carpathians, it had already been well past midnight. Accepting this as one of the stranger things that came with being friends with a demon, Jon turned to Barion.

"I enjoyed our day together very much. Would you like to come over tomorrow to play another round of *Eden's Doom*?"

Barion's smile lit up the entire apartment. "Really? Are you filming it again?"

"Only if it's okay with you. We can just play."

"No, I had fun." Barion hesitated. "Though perhaps you should first see what your subscribers say. If they think it's okay, I'd love to do another video with you."

"It's a deal." Jon wanted to say more, was even thinking about asking Barion to stay a bit longer when his cell started ringing, playing Chris de Burgh's *Don't Pay the Ferryman*. Jon groaned inwardly. "I'm sorry. I have to get this one. It's my Grann."

Barion nodded. "I understand. Family." He rolled his eyes. "See you tomorrow? Around nine? I can bring breakfast again."

Jon wanted to argue that it should be his turn to provide food, but the ringing of his cell grew more insistent. He knew it was technically impossible, but then again, so was coming back from the dead, and Grann *was* a witch queen. So he simply settled for a nod and a "Thank you" before he retrieved his phone from its place on the kitchen counter. Barion waved before slicing open the air and vanishing. Jon took the call.

"Hello, Grann."

"Don't 'hello' me, *enbesil*! You simply vanished hours ago to pop up in Europe, of all places! The ancestors were sick with worry when they couldn't find you! What have you been thinking, *lanfe ak kondanasyon*?"

Jon actually had to hold his cell away from his ear. Grann was on a roll and wouldn't stop until she had spoken her mind...in great, colorful detail. When she was finally running out of steam some ten minutes later, Jon managed to get a word in. "I'm so sorry, Grann. Barion invited me to his home in the Carpathians. It was a spontaneous thing, and I didn't think it would be a problem."

"You mean you didn't think of your poor, old Grann at all!"

Jon knew better than to contradict her in any way, be it the *poor, old Grann* comment or the fact that she was very obviously keeping magical tabs on him through the ancestors, even though he was a grown man—zombie—with a life of his own. No, contrary to what she had called him, he was no *enbesil* and knew when to keep his mouth shut.

"I'm sorry, Grann. Barion and I were just having so much fun. We played a video game together and he invited me to have pizza with me that he fetched from Rome." He was also a master in the art of distraction and had no shame in playing the cute grandchild who'd simply gotten carried away, even though it was very much the truth in this case. The heavy sigh coming through the phone told him he had at least gained some points.

"Pizza from Rome sounds nice, *cherie*." She made a pregnant pause. "This *demontre*, he treats you well?"

"He's a perfect gentleman. I like him very much."

"I see…"

Jon didn't like the tone of her voice. It was a mixture of worry, apprehension and a dose of plain fear he had never heard from her before. "Grann, is there something you're not telling me?"

Again, a sigh. "There's a great many things I'm not telling you or anybody else, for that matter, *cherie*. The world of *majik*, it's not without dangers, as you well know."

"Grann, I'm in a book club with two witches, a banshee, an ancient vampiress, two werewolves I'm pretty sure are uber alphas, and, as of late, a demon prince and his mate who once was human — and I'm a zombie. I think I'm aware of the dangers."

"Knowing Maribel and Mavis are there is what reassures me a bit." And the cryptic comments commenced. Jon didn't bother to ask how his Grann knew the two witches. The world of *majik* was not only dangerous but also quite small when it came to the power players in it. That there was no coven in Beaconville or any of the surrounding towns and cities had told Jon right from the beginning what league the two witches played in. The same went for Declan and Troy. There were no packs in the area, the next one being three counties over, its members obsessively avoiding Beaconville, even though the town would have been perfect for a pack of considerable size. Spending most of his time in front of his computers in the cellar didn't mean Jon was clueless or deaf to what was going on around him.

Even before Dre had found Sammy, supernaturals of all kinds had avoided Beaconville. There were some who passed through, but they were few and far between. Nobody ever tried to settle down. Jon wasn't entirely sure where Amber stood in banshee hierarchy—or if they even had one. Some of her comments, though, had him wondering how old she was exactly. As for Emilia, she was comparatively young when it came to years, but not when it came to power. There had been a few instances when she'd forgotten to put her shields all up and what had dripped through was enough for Jon to know that staying on her good side was a healthy life choice, though not when she insisted that *Thud!* was Terry Pratchett's best book when everybody knew it was *Small Gods*, closely followed by *Witches Abroad*.

"I just want you to be safe and happy." Grann's voice reminded Jon that he was still on the phone with her.

"I know…and I appreciate it." He cleared his throat. "Just to give you fair warning, Barion is coming over tomorrow to play with me again. It could be that we spend part of the day at his place."

"Meaning you're going to vanish again. Be careful, *cherie*. Traveling through time and space is risky."

"Don't worry. Sammy made Barion promise he wouldn't leave me stranded in some weird-ass dimension." The words were out before Jon could judge the wisdom of speaking them.

"Did he now? Your friend Sammy is smart."

"That he is, and he would make Dre get me should Barion leave me anywhere."

"I guess I can't win this. Please keep in touch, Jon. Something is going to happen. I can feel it in my bones, see it in the sky, smell it in the swamp, but I can't grasp it because those *demontre* blur my sight."

If there hadn't been the genuine worry in her voice, Jon would have said something to lighten the mood. He instinctively knew that would be wrong here.

"I will, Grann. Don't worry. I'm fine and happy and Barion is a good man. Uh, demon. He won't let anything happen to me."

"No, I guess he won't. Take care, *cherie*." Grann hung up and left Jon staring at his cell. Except for the usual guilt trip designed to make him move back to New Orleans, this call had included everything he had come to expect from a conversation with Grann—the shouting, the curses, the cryptic comments, the worry, the love. It was all there, telling Jon what a great family he had, how much they cared about him and how lucky he was. If only that were enough.

Sighing, he glanced at the clock on his microwave. It was now half past seven a.m., and he was tired and wide awake at the same time. If this was normal for hopping between time zones with a demon, he understood why Sammy sometimes looked as if he were ready to keel over if so much as the breeze of the book shop's door opening hit him. His brain insisted it was late enough to think about lying down, while his body was sure his usual evening routine of gaming, reading and chatting with his friends and fans had only just begun. Jon decided to go for a compromise and catch up on his emails as well as take a look at the comments to the video he and Barion had made.

The emails were the usual mixture of spam. *Who on earth thinks it's a good idea to offer me, of all people, life insurance?* Well, probably people who didn't know he was zombie, but still, it was simply ridiculous. He shook his head while he deleted all the crap in his inbox before he read through the few important mails, two of them from major gaming companies asking for his expertise on new games they were developing.

Jon always loved to get a look at games when they were still in the creative process and give his input, so he told them to just hit him with whatever they had. After that, he turned his attention to his and Barion's video. The comments were mostly positive. There were always a few who weren't satisfied, but then again, only a fool would try to please everybody, and he felt confident announcing a second video with Barion. Thinking about it for a moment, he decided eleven o'clock would be a good time for the next round of playing *Eden's Doom,* and he posted it on FB, Twitter and sent a short notice to his YouTube subscribers. While he checked his sale's numbers on YouTube, he watched the likes, shares, and re-tweets skyrocket within less than half an hour, which told him his fans had truly liked the video. If it was more the content or the new player remained to be seen. Jon was more than happy to give it a few more tries. After he had taken care of all the tedious little details that came with being a freelancer, he shut all his computers down except for his laptop. He was getting ready for bed and needed a little treat before he went to sleep.

When Iron Bull's scarred face filled the screen of his laptop, Jon leaned back in his ergonomic chair to enjoy the beautiful relationship between the Dom and his Kadan. Somewhere between Iron Bull telling Kadan that he could let go of everything when he was with him and Kadan giving Iron Bull the dragon's tooth, Jon replaced Iron Bull's face with that of Barion — which was much more handsome, no doubt there — and Kadan with himself. He surely looked better in such a tight pair of trousers. When Iron Bull-Barion asked Kadan-Jon to give him a minute and Jon answered that it was almost always more than a minute with him, he felt a strange stirring in his groin. It had been so long since Jon had felt anything remotely sexual that it took him a moment to place the electric feeling between his legs. He was getting hard...from fantasizing about Barion. Not sure if lusting about a friend was acceptable — Jon had a sinking feeling it was not — he hesitated.

On the one hand, this was his first real boner since he'd woken up in a coffin. On the other hand, he really liked Barion as a friend and wanted to see where their friendship would go. It was nerve-racking, and when he felt his erection fading, Jon made a quick decision. He would not miss out on having an orgasm for the first time in what felt like eons. Barion didn't have to know about it at all. What Jon did in the privacy of his rooms and in his head was entirely up to him.

Satisfied with his reasoning, Jon opened the zipper of his trousers, pushed them over his ass, together with his underwear — the Cookie Monster's face was a little distorted from being pushed outward like that — and got back into the lustful fantasy where Barion dragged him into a random empty room to cover him with his much bigger body and ravish and plunder him until he cried out in sheer lust. The strong, huge hands of the demon closed around his cock, the warmth in them sending Jon to heights he could have never dreamed of while, after some wiggling, one scorching hot digit breached his entrance, teasing the rim with just its presence. Two strong pumps and Jon came with a pained scream, his orgasm tearing out of him with an intensity he'd never felt before.

Gasping and twitching, he came down from his high, not sure if what had just happened was good or bad but utterly convinced that he wanted to do it again…and again…and perhaps again. He suddenly understood the hunger Declan and Troy sometimes spoke about when they told about their trysts with men and women alike.

What Jon had felt when he'd come was so divine that he couldn't imagine not experiencing it ever again. Still shuddering, he managed to get up on trembling legs, his trousers and underwear bunched around his thighs, restraining his movements. His hands were full of cum and some of it had splashed on his shirt, making Deadpool look as debauched as he was often depicted in fan art. Only Spiderman was missing. Jon pulled his trousers up to get to the bathroom more easily, where he got rid of all his clothes. Seconds later he was in the shower, washing off the scents of this earth-shattering orgasm, bathing in the complete relaxation it had brought him. When he finally went to bed, he was out like a light within seconds.

Chapter Eight

Barion stood in front of his bedroom mirror, trying to decide what he should wear for the next round of gaming with Jon. The black silk shirt showed off his torso nicely but was probably a bit much for just a few hours in front of a computer screen, while the T-shirt with the grumpy panda bear announcing he was awake due to unfortunate circumstances seemed too casual for doing a video, even though it couldn't be seen on screen. While he was still pondering his options, he felt the ripple announcing the arrival of somebody. In the mirror, he saw a red claw appearing out of thin air then Dre and Sammy stood in his bedroom, both of them smiling at him brightly.

"Good morning, little brother. Are you going somewhere?"

"None of your business, big bro."

"I'd go with the shirt. It makes your skin glow." Sammy was already standing in front of Barion's wardrobe, going through his things. "But you can't combine it with those jeans. You need something more informal, playful. That is, if you do another round of gaming with Jon?" He looked at Barion over the black slacks he was holding in his hands. "Because if you want to take him out, you'll need something different."

Barion shook his head. He knew there was no way out of this, and experience had taught him to just go with it, because the deceptively innocent little devil Dre called his mate would always get what he wanted in the end. For a human—a *former* human—Sammy was exceptionally good at navigating the world of *majik*, binding powerful supernaturals to him left and right.

"The plan is for just gaming and perhaps watching a movie later. But I'll be bringing breakfast."

"Oh good, we haven't eaten yet. What did you plan on getting?" Dre was snooping through Barion's drawers, pulling out the Jack Skellington socks Sammy had given Barion as a present because he had helped so much with their mating party. Barion expertly caught them, thinking wearing them was a good idea. Jon had lots of interesting T-shirts as well, so Barion didn't feel awkward wearing his own nerd stuff.

"I was thinking about croissants and coffee from Avignon. You know the bakery I'm talking about."

A happy smile appeared on Dre's lips. "The one operated by the hedgehog shifters. Great idea."

"There's hedgehog shifters?" Sammy's eyes were glowing with interest while he pushed a pair of ripped, heavily washed-out jeans into Barion's hands. It wouldn't have been his first choice, probably not a choice at all, but he trusted Sammy's fashion sense—to a certain degree.

"Oh yes, *mo grah thu*, a very nice prickle that me and Barion have known for years. How about we accompany Barion to Avignon and have breakfast there?"

"You have the best ideas, Dre. I'm so happy to be mated to the most intelligent demon in the whole world!"

Sammy was laying it on thick, and Dre was eating it up with a spoon. Barion made gagging noises to disrupt the flow of the two lovebirds or he knew they would be christening yet another part of his poor home, and if there was any sex happening here, he would be damned if he wasn't part of it, though not when Sammy and Dre went for it. That was just gross...and inappropriate. Perhaps one day... An image of Jon and him on the orange couch came to his mind unbidden, doing all kinds of funny things to the region of his groin.

Barion cleared his throat to distract himself from the direction his thoughts were taking. Time to get them all on a new subject. "Has Jon already talked to you about Milo?"

Both Dre and Sammy looked at him sharply. "What's going on? Is Milo in trouble?" Sammy sounded so worried. He really had taken the young man who tried to sacrifice him to Dre under his wing. It was further proof how utterly crazy the man was and a warning not to mess with him. Barion was convinced Sammy was able to kill somebody with kindness.

"I don't know. It's just that the first evening I spent with Jon, we ordered pizza and Milo brought it. I thought he had stopped with the deliveries to concentrate on his studies. Does he need more money?"

Sammy sighed. "I thought I was paying him enough. He can't work nights. He has to prepare for the tests to get into MIT. And he has to do this weird quiz to ensure he can get the additional scholarship. Dre, we need to do something."

The urgency in Sammy's voice almost had Barion regretting mentioning Milo's troubles. He could have solved the problem by only telling Dre or by simply giving the lad enough cash. It wasn't as if Barion was hurting for money, and upsetting Sammy was the last thing he wanted.

Dre took Sammy in his arms. "How about we talk to him when he comes in for work today, *mo grah thu*, to find out what is going on." He turned to Barion. "Thank you for telling us, little brother. I'm afraid Milo isn't one to ask for help when he needs it."

Barion shrugged, a little uncomfortable with the compliment. In his opinion, he could have done a lot more than just leave the trouble on Dre's and Sammy's doorstep. "It's fine. Just tell me if I can do anything. I've got lots of cash sitting around doing nothing. I could set up a trust for Milo? To see him through MIT?"

"That's very generous of you, Barion, but Milo is adamant on earning it all himself. He won't accept money as a present, which is actually one of the reasons we are so intent on helping him." Dre shook his head, muttering something about stubborn-ass humans and how one could only admire or kill them, perhaps both.

Barion was now fully clothed and ready to get breakfast then play a game. He nodded at Dre and Sammy. "I'm getting those croissants. Are you coming?"

Dre looked down at his mate, who was clearly worked up. "I think we'll pass this time. When we go there, I want Sammy to fully enjoy meeting the prickle and not worry about Milo or anything else. See you in Beaconville."

"See you and good luck."

* * * *

Half an hour later Barion appeared in front of Jon's apartment door. He rang the bell and waited for Jon to open it. The zombie looked gorgeous in a white sweater with a reaper bunny saying *Hippity, Hoppity, Your Soul Is My Property*, and a pair of dark blue jeans that were almost as ripped as Barion's own.

"Why are you ringing?"

"I thought that would be more polite than just popping up in your home, maybe doing something naughty." Barion waggled his brows. He had meant it as a joke, but the way Jon was avoiding his gaze made him think it wasn't far off the mark. "Wait! Were you doing something naughty? Without *me*?"

The teasing tone did what Barion had hoped. It tore Jon from whatever embarrassing thought he was caught in. He winked. "Could be. I don't know if anybody has ever told you that, but the world does not revolve around demons."

"Uh, hate to break it to you, but it actually does. Demons are the crown of creation."

"Sure. Whatever you choose to believe. Now, did you bring breakfast?"

"I did." Barion held out the paper bags with the croissants and some other pastries he hadn't been able to resist with a flourish. "And aren't you happy the crown of creation is able to hop between space like mundane creatures do with trains?"

Jon rolled his eyes and took the bags from Barion. "So glad. And I'm insanely happy this special crown of creation decided to share the perks of his existence with somebody as lowly and mundane as a zombie."

"That's who I am." Barion grinned. "And just for the record, I think you being a zombie is cool. Much better than some stupid werewolf or vampire."

"Rarer as well." Jon went to the kitchen, Barion hot on his heels.

"How do you mean that? I have to admit that I don't know much about zombies — apart from the thing with the brain, obviously. Wait! Should I have brought some brain? How rude of me not to ask. I'm sorry."

Jon waved it off. "No problem. My standing order is coming tomorrow, so I'm good. As for zombies being rare, well, there are different reasons for that." While he got some plates from a cupboard, Jon was obviously thinking about how to tackle the topic. Barion waited silently, giving his friend the space he needed. "There are different types of zombies and people often have a hard time distinguishing them, probably because of the terror involved when confronted with the living dead."

"Yeah. *The Walking Dead* was probably not the best PR for you guys."

"No." Jon shuddered a bit. "Especially because it depicts only a certain type of zombies, though definitely the worst."

"Enlighten me."

"Okay, so we have what people commonly think of when they hear the term 'zombie', which are the creatures depicted in many movies and series. They are animated corpses who are alive up to a certain definition of life but keep decomposing. Their bodies are like an old cloak that somebody wears until it's completely gone. Once the garment has vanished, the power that animated it has to return to Papa Legba's realm."

Jon was now arranging the pastries on a huge serving plate while Barion found himself hanging on his every word. He was the first to admit not to be too interested in other paranormals or learning about them. He suspected it had something to do with the knowledge that nobody out there could pose a real threat to him. Yes, there were a few witches who might be able to summon and control him, but they were few, and none of them had the means to control more than one demon at a time. And they all knew better than to challenge the wrath of the demon king by fucking with his people. Everything else, Barion could easily deal with by either slicing it to pieces, dumping it somewhere truly unpleasant and deadly or simply leaving it to stew in its own juices.

"Then we have the kind of zombies most often used by voodoo priests. They are very much like the first category, meaning they keep rotting away until they're gone, but the ugly thing about them is that their soul is chained to the corpse as the animating agent. They are fully aware what's happening and can't do anything against it, true slaves to the person who has brought them back. It isn't done very often anymore because people don't look favorably upon it, and Grann says it's too much hassle to resurrect somebody anyway. There's easier ways to get revenge, less obvious."

"Your Grann sounds like a sensible woman." Barion offered the compliment without knowing the woman, but anybody who had raised Jon had to be good. He thought about it for a moment, his brain catching up with the math after it had gotten a swift kick from his common sense.

"Wait. Your Grann? How is that possible? I know from Sammy you're at least a hundred years old."

"Uhm, a hundred and three. And it's possible because she's like me." Jon carried the plate with the pastries to the coffee table in his living room. Barion followed him with the smaller plates and the two cups of coffee he had brought with him. They both sat down, and Jon took one of the croissants, bit into it and moaned. "So good. Thank you for bringing these."

"You're welcome. Now back to your Grann and how she is like you." Barion knew he sounded impatient, but he found he wanted to find out more about Jon. The zombie looked uncertain. "You don't have to tell me anything. I'm just being pushy. We can talk about something else," Barion assured Jon when he sensed his trepidation.

Jon shook his head. "It's fine. I just haven't told anybody about this ever."

Barion realized what a big deal this was for Jon and leaned forward to touch his hand. Jon flinched automatically at the contact but didn't pull away. On the contrary, after a short moment of hesitation, he turned his palm upward to weave his fingers between Barion's. "I died of the Spanish flu in 1918 and was woken only hours later by Amede and Gaspar Honoré, Grann's grandsons, who prayed to Papa Legba to bring her back because her people were lost without her guidance. That I was wakened as well was an accident."

"Ah, yes you mentioned it when we talked about your gamer name. Now it all makes sense. The grandsons didn't intend to wake you also?"

"No. Grann lectured them for days about why performing a ritual designed to bring back the dead in a room chock-full of corpses was a *bad* idea." Jon chuckled at the memory. Now, over a hundred years later and without being occupied to try to come to terms with his new circumstances, he could see the funny side of things.

"Uh, they probably didn't think that one through." Barion was sniggering.

"No, they didn't. In their defense, they were panicking. It was the first time New Orleans had been without a witch queen or king from the Honoré line, and they were terribly afraid who would come and fill the vacant spot."

"I guess that won't ever be a worry again."

"Nope. Grann has things on a tight leash. Anyway, she and I represent the third type of zombie, the true undead. Our souls aren't chained to our bodies but have been returned of our free will—don't ask me, I don't remember giving my consent—and Papa Legba has infused our corpses with a magic similar to the one vampires have. We do not rot. We do not age. We *are*."

"You don't sound entirely happy about that."

Jon took another bite of his croissant before he answered. "I have to admit that I'm still struggling with the concept of potentially living eternally. When I died, I thought that was it, and after I came back, it took me some years to get used to being back but different. I guess it's something else for demons or other supernatural creatures like vampires and werewolves. You know from the beginning that you're looking at a very long lifespan. Back when I was human, we were very much aware of how fragile life was, especially when the flu started spreading. Making your peace with death then suddenly being back, no longer under her dominion is…unsettling."

"I can see that." Barion took a sip of his coffee. "I don't understand it, but I can see it. You know, for demons, the most important thing is to stave off boredom. Being alive is just a matter of course. We don't think much about death, unless we deal it out. Then it's frankly more along the lines of 'do I go to the trouble of covering it up' or 'do I just leave the mess here'. Sorry," he added, when he saw the look on Jon's face. The zombie waved it off.

"No, it's fine. I was a bit taken aback, but thinking about it, you're right. Different perspectives and everything."

They both ate in silence for a while. It wasn't uncomfortable. They were both thinking about what they had learned concerning the other. When they were done, Jon got up to clear the plates. Barion helped him.

"When do we start our game?"

Jon smiled and looked at the watch. "In half an hour. I announced we would go live at eleven."

"Cool. Plenty of time to get everything ready."

Chapter Nine

"And we start in five, four, three, two, go." Jon pushed the button on the remote that started the cameras and microphones. A quick glance at his side screen showed him they already had a huge audience, all of them pumped for the game, as it seemed from the comments.

"Hello, everybody, this is PLM and Big B again, with another round of *Eden's Doom*. In the last session we played the first levels, and the jury is still out on how we found them." Laughing emojis filled the comments. "Big B, have you changed your mind?"

Barion grinned at him. "Nope. I still think the first level is completely wasted. But let's see what the next ones have in store. It can only get better."

They played another two levels, and Jon had to admit the game was rather boring. The graphics were solid, as was the programming, but the entire game lacked the charm he had expected. Barion was equally unimpressed, voicing his thoughts clearly.

"Damn, this demon looks so lame...and unrealistic. I mean, please. What self-respecting demon would wear armor that tacky when going into battle? There's nothing to protect his stomach, which also happens to be one of his weak points. How is this supposed to be a real fight if the opponents have such blatant weaknesses?"

He's right.

That demon looks ridiculous.

Hey, Big B, what do you think should a demon look like?

Oh, yeah, what kind of armor would you suggest?

I don't think I'm going to buy this game.

Barion could read the comments more easily because this time Jon had set the smaller screen between the two of them to give his friend a better chance to interact with the audience. Jon nodded at him, urging him to answer the questions.

"Yes, Big B, what kind of armor would you suggest?" He grinned.

Barion leaned back, letting his angel avatar do a spinning motion to kill off the demon he had just criticized. "Well, first of all, I would protect his vulnerable parts, not that real demons have any, just saying. But the armor would be made of bewitched steel forged in one of the hell dimensions, impenetrable and with the markings of the demon's heritage on it, since he can't show them off on his skin, what with having to protect it."

Jon listened, fascinated, while Barion spun a tale of truth and fantasy, mixing the two so expertly that he had the audience eating out of his hands in no time flat. With a glance at the comments, Jon added his two cents.

"What would you do if you could design your own game, Big B? I certainly would choose a different story, and in my game, the opponents would be worth the name."

"Yeah." Barion paused the game. "I think I would model my game after the demon wars. Actually, that's what I'd name it, *Demon Wars*. And it would be demons against demons, no angels involved. They tend to solve their problems with sex rather than violence anyway. A bit like bonobos in that respect."

This guy is so funny.

Demon Wars *is a great idea! Sounds like a fun game.*

I want a game like that! PLM, can't you create a game with Big B?

Oooh, yes, that would be great. I'd certainly buy that.

Big B's ideas sound great. As if there were real demons and angels. So authentic.

Jon raised his brows at Barion, who was staring at the screen with his mouth open. Then a smile stretched his lips.

"That's actually not a bad idea at all, PLM. Let's do our own video game. I've got tons of inspiration, and you're the definition of experience. We should be able to create a killer game."

The comments exploded with encouragement, and the longer Jon thought about it, the better he thought the idea was. He did have a lot of experience, certainly to invent and program something better than this. And Barion had the entire history of his species to draw from. *This could be so much fun.*

"Fine, let's give it a try. It'll take some time, though."

The *awws* and *ooohs* from the comments had him smiling. "We want the end product to be perfect and to your liking. But we will get your input during different stages of the process. How does that sound?"

There was a cascade of cheers in the comments. Barion put his hand on Jon's and the touch was very welcome, much to his never-ending surprise.

"Well, then, fellow gamers, we have work to do! See you soon and happy gaming!" Jon cut the camera and turned to Barion. "Looks as if we have a game to create."

Barion appeared to be a bit dazed. "Are you fine? Would you rather we don't do this?"

The demon shook his head. "No, I love the idea. It's just...wow. That's the first time in centuries that I have a real project, you know, not just goofing around. We are serious about this, aren't we?"

"Totally. To be honest, I'm hyped. All these years, I've just commented on games. Building one myself from scratch feels good." Jon got up from his place on the couch, craning his neck left and right to work out the kinks. "Tell me about the demon wars?"

Barion leaned back, putting the keyboard down. "Uh, well, I could, you know, show them to you?" He was looking very intently at his fingers. Jon furrowed his forehead.

"What do you mean, show them to me? Are they still ongoing? Where? And I'm not sure I want to be on a battlefield."

"No, no, the demon wars ended roughly two thousand years ago. It's..." He fell silent, wiggled on the couch, grabbed the keyboard, put it down again. Jon got the feeling that Barion was nervous and Jon didn't understand why.

"Hey, Barion, if this is going too fast, I understand. We can let it go for today, sleep over it, if you want."

"That's not it." Barion sighed. "You see, demons have secrets—lots of them, actually—and even though we haven't known each other for long, I feel compelled to tell you one of mine, and it makes me all worked up."

Jon sat back down next to Barion, putting his hand on the demon's forearm. The heat tingled through his fingertips, traveled into his body and made him feel more alive than he had been before he died. "Barion, you don't have to share your secrets with me if you don't feel comfortable about it. I agree that we haven't known each other for long, and I, too, feel the need to involve you more in my life and history than I normally would after such a short time. I swear to you that whatever you're going to tell me is safe with me. I won't ever betray your confidence." Jon chuckled. "Besides, who would I tell? I assume Dre and Sammy know, and while I do meet the others regularly in the book club, I'll hardly get up and say something like, *Oh, and by the way, did you know...*while we're discussing male stereotypes in *Huckleberry Finn*."

Barion laughed. "Okay, if you put it like that."

"I do put it like that."

"It's not that I don't trust you. You know that, don't you?"

Jon nodded.

"Then here we go. Additionally to our very impressive powers and skills, every demon of the royal family has a special talent they inherit through the mother's line. We guard those talents closely, even though they're usually not that impressive, more like party tricks. It's a tradition."

"And where would we end if we didn't respect tradition, even if we don't know how they originated anymore?" Jon grinned.

"Exactly. Anyway, my talent is... There's not really a name for it. Dre calls it 'time bending', though that's a big word for the five minutes I can actually bend."

"You mean going back and forth?" Jon was fascinated and a little jealous. It seemed every supernatural had something cool up their sleeves while zombies were...undead. Just that. It was unfair, really.

"Yeah. I honestly don't know if there are beings who can manipulate time on a larger scale, though Quirion doubts it. He said five minutes is probably the longest span possible, because everything before it is already cast in stone and everything after offers too many variables to grasp it with even the most powerful magic."

"Sounds logical. How does it work?"

"If you were to go over there and, let's say, drop that plate, I can step between the, the, what does Quirion call them? Ah, yes, the event horizons leading to the plate falling, skip them and catch it before it smashes."

"You freeze time?" Jon wasn't sure he'd understood Barion correctly.

"No. Not as such. Think of it as cheating. You can't really freeze time, because it always moves, like a river. But in a river, there are rocks, and with rocks, you can build little dams, which is basically what I do. I buy myself time to be there when the event takes place."

"I think I'm getting a headache." Jon shook himself. "Wait a moment. When you and Dre open those rifts, you always call it traveling through time and space. Now you say you can't manipulate time beyond those five minutes and that the others can't do it at all?"

Barion looked puzzled. "We do travel through time and space, like everybody who gets into a car to drive from point A to B or when you go up into Sammy's shop. The demon way of travel is just fancier, like everything demons do."

"So you can't leave me in time? Like Sammy said last time?"

"Uh, no and yes. No, I can't dump you, let's say in the Middle Ages, because I don't have access to time that has been used already."

"But?"

"But what?"

Jon rolled his eyes. "Your tone suggests a huge 'but' and you said 'no and yes'. I'm curious what the 'yes' entails."

"You're a smart one, aren't you?" Barion grinned.

"You only realize that now? The yes?"

Barion tapped his index finger against his lips, clearly thinking for a moment. "In order to travel demon style, you have to change the shape of space. Time and space are…connected — not in a way that's logical for a non-demon, but the connection is there. So, if I left you — and I want to stress very strongly, that I would *never* do that — in a rift in transition, so to speak, you would technically be lost in time, even though time as such isn't even a component of the rift. Neither is space, but you need non-space and non-time to hop around dimensions. I'm not making any sense to you, am I?"

"What gave me away?"

"The glazed-over look in your eyes was a strong indicator."

"Damn, you got me." Jon winked, not the least bit upset about not understanding, because he could see Barion had tried his best to be clear. Jon had the strong suspicion one had to be a demon to really get it. "Since I don't think there's any hope of me understanding demonic travel any better than Amber does baking, why don't we get back to your talent, which I think is super cool, by the way."

Barion bowed with a flourish. "Thank you. The really cool thing about my talent is that, even though I can't manipulate time beyond said five minutes, I can replay it, like a DVD."

Jon's eyes went wide. "*All* of it?"

"*All* of it." Barion preened like a peacock.

"Holy shit."

"Yep. Do you want to see?" The big demon seemed like an eager puppy.

"Of course I want to see. How about I prepare us some snacks and we get comfortable on the couch? Do you need anything? Like a screen?"

"No. Just the snacks. You want to see anything in particular?"

"The demon wars, of course. Let's not forget we have a game to create."

Barion saluted. "Demon wars coming up."

Jon went to the kitchen where he put chips into a bowl, found some pretzels and a sour cream dip which he arranged more or less artfully on a plate, before he poured them both water from the fridge. It wasn't what humans would think of as healthy, but Barion was an immortal demon and Jon already dead. Being able to basically eat whatever he fancied was one of the few things about his undead existence that Jon had embraced from the very beginning. Once they were comfortable on the couch, Jon looked at Barion expectantly.

"What are you going to show me?"

"I've been thinking about it, and I believe the Battle at Ch'tal'ur is a good starting point. It has everything from close range fighting inside a building to an open battlefield and a chase through the woods."

"Sounds interesting already. Who is fighting against whom?"

Barion cocked his head. "Uh, everybody against everybody else?"

"I'm not sure I'm following."

They stared at each other for a moment, both wondering about what the other was thinking. It was Jon who tried to resolve the matter.

"I meant, what are we looking at? Is it the Targaryens against the Lannisters or House Stark against House Tyrell?"

Understanding dawned on Barion's face. "I see… I should have explained better." He cleared his throat. "In demon society, there are no houses. There's just the royal family, of which I'm part, as you can see from my silver markings" — he gestured at the intricate silver tattoos on his blue skin where they were visible on his forearms and neck — "and the warrior caste, who have bronze tattoos. Normal demons have black markings, though that doesn't make them any less dangerous. Only the king, my father, has gold markings, and should he ever decide to hand the mantle over to one of us" — Barion shuddered visibly — "his markings will turn to silver while those of the next king will change to gold."

Jon was fascinated. "Did that happen when your father became king?"

"Yes. Grandfather was fed up with the constant fighting around the time the dinosaurs walked the Earth. According to him, it took some serious bribing to convince Father to take on the burden."

"Your father has been the king of all demons since the *Jurassic period*?"

"Yeah. He says the Earth was more fun back then because demons could walk around freely."

Jon felt his head spin and decided to return to the original topic before they got lost in what seemed to be complicated family dynamics a *long* time in the making. "Demons have different markings, though that doesn't make them more or less dangerous. Got it. Has your father ever been challenged?"

"You mean challenged for the position of having to oversee a vast bunch of immortal creatures with the patience of a two-year-old toddler and the destructive power of several atomic bombs? Strangely enough, nobody has *ever* tried to wrestle the crown from him."

Jon could see the logic in that. Still… "Then why did the demon wars happen? They're over, aren't they?"

"In most universes, yes, especially here because we've realized humans are much more fun alive." Barion winked. "And the wars happened because demons get bored quickly and we're not exactly built for crafting to pass time." He held up one of his huge hands, slowly letting the claws slide free. Though 'claws' was probably not the right word for the sword-like appendages with the very pointy, very sharp ends. "What we *are* good at is fighting and destroying things. Hence the wars." Barion must have seen something in Jon's eyes because he spoke on a bit hastily. "When I say war, I don't mean it in the same way you do."

Jon arched a brow. "Let's see. In a war people fight against each other with whatever weapon they have at hand, with the goal to kill as many enemies as possible and come out the winner, who is usually determined by the amount of land or riches or power he or she has amassed."

"That would be a human war, yes. Very accurate." Barion took a sip from his water. "With demons, the first problem is they are indestructible, so killing is off the table. The second is that we only tolerate close family but usually no other demons, unless they turn out to be our mate. Between demons there are no alliances. Everybody is on their own."

"You just said you tolerate close family."

"Do you have siblings?"

Jon opened his mouth and closed it again. After a moment, he said, "I see. No reason for the fight, combatants are invincible and bored, so it's all in good fun?"

"You got it!" Barion beamed.

"Who do I cheer for in the fight you're going to show me?"

"Whoever you want. Though the overall consent is that my great-aunt from Dre's mother's side, Augnielle, had the most beautiful form that day."

"I'm cheering for Augnielle." Jon leaned back on the sofa and took some chips while Barion did something with his hand. His claws were still out, creating a strange silvery effect in the air, making it shimmer as if it were a hot day. The waves of that shimmer expanded and all of a sudden Jon was sitting in the middle of a spirited fight and had a green demon with black markings running toward him, claws out, wings spread, incredibly sharp teeth bared.

"Holy shit!" Jon tried to sink into the cushions of his couch when the demon simply ran through him, causing not even a ripple in the air.

"Are you okay?" Barion sounded worried.

"Fine. I'm fine. Just wasn't expecting to be in the middle of it all." When the next demon, a black one with bronze markings, came stomping from the side, Jon was ready. It was intercepted by another demon, this one purple with bronze tattoos, who Jon thought could maybe be female. The scales looked a bit better groomed, like the owner took the time to oil them. Then again, manscaping was a thing, and who said male demons didn't oil their scales? Jon glanced at Barion, wondering if this was something he could ask his friend or if he was crossing a line.

"That's Augnielle," Barion offered.

At least he had guessed right. Jon watched as the purple demon sidestepped the black one, whirled around with her wings close to her body and rammed her claws into the other demon's side. He screamed, if in pain or outrage was hard to tell, though Jon was leaning toward pain the moment he saw the blue blood gushing from the wound.

"I thought you said demons are invincible?"

"Uhm, they are. See? The wounds are already healing." Barion pointed at the demon whose wounds were indeed closing at a rapid speed. A few moments later, only the blue blood splatter indicated he had been wounded. With a roar, he threw himself back into battle.

The fighting went back and forth, and Jon would have lost track of things if Barion hadn't provided him with additional info now and then. What he did learn quickly was that Barion had been right — modelling a video game after the demon wars could be a great success if done right. They would have to do some thinking on proper armor — apparently demons didn't need it because their skin was thicker than anything that could be forged and their claws sharp enough to cut even through their skin—but that would be part of the fun of mixing reality with fiction, not that their audience would ever know. And just from the hour or so of what Barion had showed him, Jon was brimming with ideas for different levels and quests. His excitement must have been contagious or Barion simply was as hyped as he was because they spent over five hours planning the game, doing some rough sketches of a few of the avatars, Augnielle being the model for one of the fiercest. At seven in the evening, Barion got some pizza from Florence, and after they had eaten, they both slumped on the couch, mentally exhausted and with their bellies pleasantly filled. The silence between them was companionable, nothing Jon felt compelled to break.

After a while, Jon wasn't sure if he hadn't dozed off a little, Barion cleared his throat.

"I don't know about you, but I'm kind of beat. How about we watch something light and call it a night?"

"Sure. We were super creative today. We've earned ourselves a little treat. What do you suggest?"

Barion grinned wickedly. Waving his hand, this time with sheathed claws, the air started shimmering again. A well-known scarred face appeared in front of the couch, the body of Iron Bull almost as big as Jon imagined it would be in real life—if the characters from *Dragon Age* were real.

"I thought you can only show the past?" He raised a brow. Barion leaned back on the couch, crossing his hands behind his head.

"Somebody played the Iron Bull romance *in the past* and put it on YouTube. That means I can show it."

"I'm so glad you're my friend." Jon looked at the huge form of Iron Bull and his much smaller Kadan, the characters appearing so real standing inside his living room and not confined to a screen. It was as if they were part of their personal peep show, and Jon started feeling the by-now-familiar stirrings in his lower body. He gulped. As happy as he was about his newly awakened libido, getting a boner in front of his friend was not—

From the corner of his eye, he saw Barion fidgeting where he was sitting. The front of his jeans showed an impressive bulge. Huge. Inviting. Calling to Jon and his urges. He felt drool gathering in his mouth. This was wrong, so wrong, but, oh, so beautiful, the way the denim stretched under the force of Barion's erection. It was a thing of such beauty that Jon thought he should probably write a poem about it. He'd never written one before, but with such inspiration, how hard could it be? It would be something about flesh fighting against the confines of cloth, about the triumph of beauty and lust over common sense, about wanting something so badly it hurt inside his chest. Jon placed a hand on where his heart had once beaten, the emotions inside him a whirlwind he wasn't able to stop.

Barion must have sensed him watching, because he slowly turned his head.

Their gazes met. Jon thought he ought to feel embarrassed, sporting an erection in front of a friend and now business partner, and being caught. As if Barion could see right into his head where all those naughty images of Barion naked, of Barion holding Jon down, of Barion taking what he wanted and giving Jon everything he needed, were running in an endless loop. Luckily, all he saw in Barion's eyes was the same heat he was feeling. Jon realized his breath was coming faster, matching the rapid rise and fall of his demon friend's chest.

In front of the sofa, Iron Bull explained to Kadan that his watchword would be 'stop'. Jon's jeans became uncomfortably tight when pictures of Barion telling him his watchword overlayed the hulky figure of Iron Bull.

Barion made a low, groaning sound, his huge hand hovering above his bulge, red bleeding into his eyes. Jon wasn't sure if it was the lighting, but he also thought the demon had grown, was now closer to his true form. He was definitely broader in the shoulders. *Bigger and broader than Iron Bull. And a lot sexier as well.*

"Stop looking at me like that. You're killing me," Barion groaned. "Is this okay?" The demon's hand went down to his zipper, fumbling for it, hesitating. He looked up, the red in his eyes a fierce glow, like lava spilling from a volcano. He was giving Jon a chance to tell him this was going too far, that it was inappropriate, that he felt uncomfortable —

Jon couldn't keep his gaze from Barion's zipper while his shaking hands reached for his own. He didn't know what was going on, if this was a good idea or appropriate between friends. All he knew was that the fire burning through his veins needed an outlet and that Barion was offering something Jon had been dreaming of more and more frequently since he'd met the demon. His voice was nothing more but a croaking sound.

"Very okay."

With a relieved sigh, Barion opened his zipper and the button, letting his cock spring free. It was even more impressive than Jon had guessed. He felt more drool forming in his mouth. *What a thing of beauty.* His own zipper put up a bit of a fight, but he was victorious when Iron Bull laid down with his Kadan.

Jon couldn't remember if he'd ever been so easily, quickly and intensely aroused when he was still alive. He blamed it on the combination of what was becoming his favorite jerk-off material and the literally and figuratively hot demon sitting on the same sofa with him, who had been invading his dreams lately. He heard Barion hissing something in a language Jon didn't recognize. His friend had his hand wrapped around his monstrous cock and was pumping it lazily, his red eyes focused on Jon's groin.

For a brief moment, Jon wondered why he didn't feel intimidated or inadequate when confronted with such an abundance of masculinity. He quickly realized it was because of the bond he felt between himself and Barion. They were a good team, friends. There was no reason to be cowed and a lot of reason to admire. Barion was willing to share this intimate moment with him, to show himself in a way he wouldn't do with just anybody. They were equals in this, no matter the differences in their bodily appearance.

Relief swept through Jon, and he shoved his hand down the waistband of his boxers, dragging his own shaft outside. A low whine came from Barion, accompanied by more frantic pumping. The sound of skin being rubbed made Jon's cock twitch against his stomach. He grabbed his erection, his gaze traveling between Barion's burning eyes and leaking member, not knowing what he found more captivating.

It took him a moment to find the same rhythm as Barion, but once he did, the air between them seemed to thicken even more. Jon thought he could feel electricity sparking between them, and they each turned their body slightly toward the other.

The pumping grew more frantic to the sounds of Kadan telling Iron Bull that with him, it was never just a minute. Jon almost laughed at that. He was so close, and it would be a miracle if he made it another thirty seconds. His balls were drawing up, getting hard, the tingling in his spine was increasing. Barion gasped, gripping his cock harder, making a twisting motion with his hand that had him arching up his spine, lifting his ass off the couch.

The visual alone was enough. Jon started shooting his load into his hand. He was still stroking frantically, riding out wave after wave of the most intense orgasm he'd ever had. Next to him, Barion wasn't faring any better it seemed, the demon grunting and groaning, his lower body still rigid in the air above the sofa, showcasing all those gorgeous muscles. The pungent smell of cum filled the air, caused Jon's cock to give a last, weak spurt.

He slumped back on the couch, his hand sticky, his cock going limp. Barion was in a similar pose, still covering his own member with his hand. In front of them, Iron Bull was asking his Kadan to dance.

"Wow. That was—" Jon didn't know how to describe his moment of pure ecstasy.

"Better than anything I've ever felt." Barion looked at him. "Thank you."

"What are you thanking me for? It was great."

"Are we still friends?" Now Barion sounded insecure. Jon thought about it. Could he be friends with somebody he had jerked off with? Was that a thing? The answer came as easy as breathing—with Barion, everything was possible.

"Of course we are. If you still *want* to be my friend?" Suddenly Jon felt nervous, not knowing if Barion felt the same way he did. He shouldn't have worried.

"Very much!" Barion said hastily.

"Oh, good." Jon grinned. "I wouldn't have known what to call us now anyway. Friends with benefits doesn't really fit, I think."

Barion chuckled. "Neither does fuck buddies. 'Friends' is good. Friends can jerk off together to their favorite virtual romance. Totally appropriate."

"Who are you trying to sell on this?"

"Both of us?" Barion turned serious. "I don't want things to change between us. I like what we have, and I'd love to keep seeing you, working with you."

"Me too. Friends it is." Jon chuckled. "I'd offer to shake hands with you, but no."

"No, not at the moment. Let's get cleaned up."

Barion went to the guest bathroom and Jon into the one attached to his bedroom. After they were both cum free, they spent another hour on the couch, this time watching the first two episodes of *The Big Bang Theory* to calm down. When Barion left, Jon was so content, he fell asleep almost immediately.

Chapter Ten

"How's my favorite little brother doing?" Dre popped into Barion's living room with a broad grin on his face. Barion stared at him with bleary eyes. It had been a tough week. He and Jon had fleshed out the background story for *Demon Wars*, deciding on the characters, their weaponry and the first few levels. This had included endless hours of watching the real demon wars to come up with suitable scenarios. Today they wanted to go on a little tour through some of the less deadly hell dimensions. *Is there a thing as 'less deadly'?* Barion wasn't sure. *Dead is dead, after all.* Then again, Jon was dead and still alive, and he wasn't sure what ghosts were. Before he got his sleepy brain into a knot, he decided that Quirion, their oldest brother, was the one for the philosophical questions. Anyway, he didn't have time to deal with Dre because he needed to get to Jon.

He wanted to take him to his favorite diner in some tiny village in Canada where they made the best pancakes ever before they started with their excursion.

And they would need the fuel. The hell dimensions could take it out of a person, especially when said persons wanted to indulge in their favorite after-work activity later that day. Barion would have never thought jerking off with another man could be so erotic. Just seeing the expression on Jon's face when he got close to climax was—

"Ahem." Dre coughed loudly into his fist, drawing Barion's attention. "I was asking how my favorite little brother was doing?"

"Don't be ridiculous. I'm your *only* little brother."

"Still my favorite."

"Where's the menace, aka your beloved mate?" Barion decided it was better to change the topic. The last shouting match with Dre had lasted for over a week of *"No, I didn't!"*, *"The hell you did!"* ending in an uneasy truce after Alerion had forced them to say their sentences at the exact same time so neither of them had the last word. Barion still knew, in his heart of hearts, that he had been right. Dre *had* eaten the last piece of Zenobia's famous lemon cake. He was just too much of a coward to own up to it.

"Sammy is at home trying to talk Milo into accepting our money to go to MIT. The stubborn idiot is refusing."

"You found out why he started doing pizza delivery again?"

Dre's expression turned grim. "We did. His mother's got cancer. They found it early. It's a miniscule knot in her right breast and the prognosis is stellar, but the costs are abominable. Her insurance doesn't cover everything, and there are some things her physicians strongly recommend that are simply too expensive for her to pay. Milo is trying to make as much money as possible, which means studying for the entrance test to MIT has become his second priority."

"Fuck. Can't Sammy simply pay him more?"

"We tried that. The boy isn't stupid. He knows Sammy is already paying him a much higher wage than is usual for the kind of job he's doing. He flat out refuses to accept a raise." Dre sounded so frustrated and Barion could relate. It was good to have some pride, but Milo was being ridiculous about it. Barion also knew it wouldn't be a good idea to tell Milo that to his face.

"He does realize the money you're offering is just sitting around, not doing anything except attracting more of its kind?"

"He does. He says he wants to earn it. Problem is, where does a high school student get a job that's paying enough to support his sick mother while leaving him enough time to study for his entrance test?"

Barion wasn't sure if it was the wording of Dre's question or something else, but he had an epiphany. "Quirion!"

"What about him? Are you hoping he could talk some sense into Milo?" Dre rubbed his temples. "Hmm, not a bad idea. The way Quirion can go on and on, Milo will probably beg us to give him money just so our brother stops talking to him. It reeks a bit of blackmail, but it could work." Dre lifted his hand in preparation to slice space and time. Barion shook his head.

"No, I didn't mean it that way, though it could be our plan B."

"Then what did you mean?"

"Quirion always moans about how much work it is to keep track of all his books. And since he won't let Sammy anywhere near his library again, Milo is the perfect candidate. He knows his way around books because of his work for Sammy, and Quirion's library is in one of the more dangerous dimensions, which means Milo is entitled to hazard pay, even though the library itself is perfectly safe, and of course the basic wage has to be quite high as well, since he has to put up with Quirion."

"That actually sounds sensible, though I still don't understand why Quirion made such a fuss. Sammy was only trying to help."

Barion loved his brother dearly, but the pout on his lips was simply ridiculous and his inability to see Sammy's faults—few as there were—had made for a very interesting afternoon in Quirion's home. Barion had been sure his ears were going to bleed out his brain if his brother and brother-in-law wouldn't stop discussing the different ways of storing books to find them as easily as possible. As it turned out, Sammy liked to order his books first by field, then by alphabet while Quirion preferred to have them all by alphabet— not to mention that Sammy alphabetized them by author while Quirion liked to do it by title, a disagreement that for some time threatened to end in blood and tears. Finally, the argument had gotten so heated that Barion had felt the need to give his two cents to calm the situation down. Needless to say, the two had then decided to team up against him, because apparently, storing the books with the wrong system was still preferable to just putting them on a shelf. Barion had fled the scene quickly, and so far, Dre and Sammy hadn't been invited back to Quirion's home, which was, essentially, the library.

"Sure, brother. Don't forget that Quirion is older than us and set in his ways. The discussion did him good, though. I haven't seen him so lively in ages."

"Yeah, he was all riled up."

They grinned at each other, reveling in the memory of seeing their usually unflappable brother with his panties in a knot. Sammy had definitely brought some fresh air into the family.

"He and Sammy are writing each other letters," Dre confessed.

"You mean they email each other."

"No. They do it the old-fashioned way — with expensive paper and real ink and using quills. Sammy has learned calligraphy just so he and Quirion can keep arguing in written form about libraries and how to organize them. They even seal their letters with wax." Dre stared at him, wide-eyed. "I absolutely don't get it, but they're both happy."

"Whatever floats their boats." Barion shrugged. He had long ago given up on understanding their oldest brother. Dre, he could get, but Quirion? He was so un-demon like that it was spooky...unless his books were threatened, then Barion steered clear of him. He loved a good brawl like every demon, but Quirion in one of his moods? That wasn't a brawl. It was slaughter.

"Are you going to talk to him? About Milo working for him?"

"Definitely." Dre let his claws spring free. "I'm doing it right now. Keep your fingers crossed that this is a solution Milo can accept. And thank you for the idea."

"You're welcome." Barion felt oddly content about having provided the possible solution to this problem.

Having a family was a pain in the ass most of the time but could be quite rewarding as well.

When Dre was gone, Barion checked his outfit—sturdy jeans, older T-shirt that could get dirty, wet, burned or simply shredded and biker boots made from thick leather. *Perfect*. He was ready for their little trip to the hell dimensions. He sliced space and time and popped up in Jon's living room. His friend had told him it wasn't necessary for him to appear outside the apartment and ring the bell because of all the time they spent together in Jon's basement apartment. Jon was already dressed in clothes similar to the ones Barion was wearing. He grinned happily.

"Good morning, Barion."

"Good morning, Jon. Ready to have breakfast and tackle the hell dimensions?"

"More than ready." Jon held up his backpack. "I've got something to drink, a few snacks, my cell, the new video camera to make pictures and films, and pen and paper for spontaneous ideas."

"You're such a good little boy scout. Let's get going." Barion opened time and space again and Jon stepped next to him, under his arm, as had become his habit since they had started hanging out together. Having the zombie so close to him reminded Barion of all the sexual delights they would be sharing later, and he shivered in anticipation.

They re-appeared behind the small diner with the inviting blue and gold paint on the walls. Barion had found it some forty years ago when he had been hopping around the planet randomly. The owner, a then-young native woman named Waaseyaa, had been busy skinning a rabbit at the back of the diner. Not fazed in the least by a blue-hued demon suddenly appearing right in front of her—she was a spiritual leader to her people and knew her way around the paranormal world—she had invited him to have some of her pancakes. Barion had eaten until he thought he would explode. For a brief moment he had wondered if that had been Waaseyaa's plan from the beginning and if his hide would end up on the wall next to the head of the Wapiti. He'd paid her generously for her hospitality, becoming one of her regulars. Back then, Waaseyaa had just taken over the diner from the former owner, who had retired. There were a lot of necessary repairs for which Barion had paid. The young shaman was about as stubborn as Milo and had insisted on giving Barion a share of the place. The debt had been long paid, the place was running successfully, even though it was so well hidden, and Barion was enjoying his role of favorite patron.

He led Jon around the diner to the front where they entered the cozy-looking place, leaving the still-biting cold outside. Waaseyaa spotted them immediately, hurrying around the counter with her arms outstretched in welcome and a warm smile on her face. She wore black jeans, a tunic with some spell woven into it and comfy-looking leather shoes. There was some silver in her once-raven-black hair, but her face was still that of the young woman Barion had met so many years ago.

"Barion, so good to see you!" She barreled into him, her arms going around his waist. After a moment of fierce hugging, Waaseyaa leaned back to look at Jon. "Welcome to you, too, friend of Barion." She held out her hand, which Jon took with visible reluctance. Although he had no problem being touched by Barion, other people, especially humans, seemingly still made him nervous. "It is an honor to see a returner from the spirit world."

Jon looked at her blankly for a moment, then apparently understanding dawned and he nodded. "Yes, Papa Legba was generous."

"Ah, the big black cock. I've seen him on some of my walks." She winked at Jon. "He's quite impressive, isn't he?"

"Uh, I guess."

Waaseyaa seemed to sense Jon's unease because she clapped her hands. "Let me guess... You're here for some of my famous pancakes?"

"Not just some, my dear. We need lots of fuel for our little expedition." Barion winked at Jon.

"You're traveling?" Waaseyaa was leading them to the table closest to the counter where she motioned for them to sit down. The diner was empty, normal for this late in the morning. The morning crowd rushed it between five and seven. Now, at eight, things had calmed.

"Yes. We need to check out one of the hell dimensions for inspiration." Barion beamed at her.

Waaseyaa furrowed her brows. "Those are not safe, Barion. You know that. Can your friend even withstand the climate there?" Her voice was full of worry.

"My friend's name is Jon. Sorry for not introducing him immediately. Your hug has distracted me. And I'm not taking him to the hell dimensions that are mid-cycle. Just to one in transit."

"That's better, though still not safe." Barion didn't miss the hint of steel in her voice.

"Uh, excuse me?" Jon looked at her. "What exactly does 'in transit' mean? Barion, you've been awfully vague about where we're going today and I'm getting the impression it's not as harmless as you made it sound."

Damn Jon and his perceptiveness.

Waaseyaa glared at Barion. "You haven't told him?"

"I did. I just didn't go into too much detail because first, that would have taken forever and we don't have that much time because we have a game to create, and second, because there's nothing I can't protect him from."

"You mean you wanted to play his hero?" Waaseyaa wasn't stupid either.

"Is that true? You wanted to fight the enemy for me?" Jon asked.

Barion squirmed a bit. "Yes?"

"To stand firm against all adversaries?"

"Uhm..."

"So you could, at the end of the day, relinquish all control in my arms?" Jon cocked an eyebrow in question, but there was a heated gleam in his eyes that made Barion's regret about not having told his friend more about the potential danger of their trip evaporate like spittle on a stone in the middle of the desert.

"Too obvious?"

"No. I love for us to have our own Iron Bull romance." Jon frowned. "But you need a better watchword than just 'stop'."

"What's an 'Iron Bull'?" Waaseyaa looked at them with small eyes. "Some spirit I need to know about? And what's a 'watchword'?"

Barion felt the heat in his body rising. Jon was very interested in his fingernails all of a sudden.

"I'm waiting, Barion." Waaseyaa had crossed her arms.

Barion raked his brain how to get out of that one and finally gave up. "Iron Bull is a fictitious character in a video game, not a spirit, and both Jon and I love his story. We were talking about that."

Waaseyaa stared at him as if she wanted to dissect his soul, which she was probably doing. One never knew with her. Then she started giggling. "It's about sex! I should have known. It's always about sex. I assume the watchword has to do with sex as well?"

Seeing the twinkling in her eyes, Barion knew she was yanking his chain. Waaseyaa was well versed in the ways of the world.

"It does. Happy?" He tried to end the conversation as quickly as possible. Waaseyaa shrugged.

"Not entirely, but I'm going to get some more thrills later. Now you need your pancakes so you can live out that fantasy of yours. Is it even a fantasy or more like role-playing? Cosplay? No, you're not dressed properly." She shook her head and left for the kitchen.

Jon stared at him with wide eyes. "What does she think of us?"

"Trust me, you don't want to know. Enjoy the pancakes. Everything else is the price you pay for their deliciousness."

Jon took two knives and forks from the plate in the middle of the table, handing one to Barion. "Now tell me about hell dimensions 'in transit'."

"You remembered that, huh?"

"I did." They stared at each other for some time, both trying not to laugh. Barion lost it when Jon's lip started twitching. When Waaseyaa brought them two huge plates stacked with pancakes that were a little larger than the ones usually served in the US, they were still chuckling. Barion's belly ached. He felt so happy that he could have cried.

After thanking Waaseyaa, Jon took his first forkful of golden-brown fluffy heaven. The moan coming from his lips had Barion's cock plumping.

"Did I promise too much?"

"No. These are beyond delicious. There needs to be a new word to describe how heavenly they taste." Jon took another bite. "Just the right consistency — the sugar is perfectly balanced with the butter, and it's real butter, I taste, isn't it? And don't get me started on the berry compote." The zombie rolled his eyes in ecstasy.

"It's homemade." Barion took his own bite, relishing the sweet breakfast. They ate in silence until their worst hunger was sated. Then Jon looked at him again.

"Hell dimensions in transit?"

"Oh, yes. You do know there's more than one hell, don't you?"

Jon nodded, licking some berry compote from the corner of his mouth, effectively distracting Barion. "Dre told me a bit about all the different dimensions and how most of them are uninhabitable."

"Yes. Not all hostile dimensions are hell dimensions, though."

"What's the difference?"

"Dimensions that were at some point inhabitable or will be so again sometime in the future are not considered hell dimensions. Only those realms that are truly and always hostile to all things alive carry that title."

"And you're going to take me there?"

"To one in transit, yes. You can imagine hell dimensions like big pendulums. They oscillate from one extreme to the other, either so hot you burn the moment you enter them or so cold that you freeze at the spot."

"Barion, you're not endearing me to this trip at all."

"Hear me out." Barion lifted his hands, waving them around with his fork and knife. "Every pendulum has to pass the quiescent point on its way from one extreme to the other, right?"

Jon nodded slowly.

"The same goes for hell dimensions. They're either hot or cold, two extremes at the two opposing points of its oscillation." Barion put down his cutlery. He raised his index fingers, holding them shoulder width apart, illustrating the two possible states a hell dimension usually was in. Jon hung on his every word and Barion couldn't help but puff up in pride. "Now, on the way from hot to cold or vice versa, the hell dimension experiences a state where both extremes cancel each other out. The quiescent point."

"Which is the moment I can visit?"

"Exactly!" Barion beamed. His friend was so smart!

"And how do you know it's safe for me?"

"Easy. I do a quick peak before I let you through." Barion had it all planned out.

"And how long does this balanced state last?"

"Depends on the shape time has in that dimension. Can be anything from mere seconds to several hundred years."

"And how do you know?" Jon was done with his pancakes and scraping the last of the compote from his plate.

"I'm taking you to one I've visited before and where I'm sure the transit point lasts for years. I'm not irresponsible with your safety."

"Because if you lost me, Sammy would be on your ass." Jon winked.

"Yeah, only because of Sammy. It has nothing to do with me really liking you. Nothing at all."

"I'm relieved to hear you have a healthy fear of Sammy." Jon cocked his head to the side, grinning broadly. Barion felt the next laugh bubbling up in his chest.

Waaseyaa came to get their empty plates, basking in their praise. "Now off you go to wherever you're headed." She took a step back from the table. "And I would hurry if I were you, because the spirit plane is filling up with people not liking your plan."

Jon's shoulders slumped. "That would be my family. Thank you for the warning."

She shrugged. "I told them I trusted Barion. For some reason, they weren't convinced. Said something about him taking you away to Europe?"

"Uh, yes, a long story and not really that interesting. Thanks for the pancakes, Waaseyaa. It was a pleasure, as always. See you." Barion blew a kiss in her direction, infusing it with just enough heat that she would feel it on her skin. The magic absorbed into her body, merging with her own. It wasn't something he did regularly, giving other magical creatures a taste of his own powers, but Waaseyaa was special, and she had been friendly to Jon. Besides, she always refused payment for the food she gave him. It was only fair. She smiled broadly at him.

"Thank you, Barion—though it wasn't necessary, as you know."

"Which is the reason I gave it to you." He took Jon's hand to lead him out of the diner. His friend looked around.

"Can we go, like *now*? If the spirits are congregating, it's only a question of time until Grann calls. And you know I'll have to take it then she'll forbid the trip."

Barion didn't waste time with an answer. Having been with Jon for several weeks now, he understood the very real threat Grann posed on their activities — or at least those she deemed unsafe. Therefore, Barion sliced the air and tugged Jon into the rift the exact moment his cell started humming in preparation of an incoming call. The sound died immediately when they were inside the rift, the space where time and space didn't exist — and wasn't it stupid that there were no cool names for these phenomena, because humans didn't know about them and demons never bothered with descriptions, except for 'dead', 'probably dead', 'interesting to kill', 'already killed' and 'too small to bother to kill'.

He stepped out onto a cliff that was overlooking a huge sea of red and green stones expanding to the horizon where several celestial bodies hung around like balloons. The temperature was colder than the last time he'd been there, a sure sign that the dimension was on its way to the next cold phase but not colder than it had been in Canada. He pulled Jon out of the rift but left it open in case they had to make a hasty retreat.

"Wow. This looks...wild." Jon did a full turn but made sure he stayed close to Barion.

"Yes, I know. Imagine the levels we could create with such a backdrop!"

Jon was already fumbling with his backpack, getting the video camera out they had bought for exactly this purpose. He started filming the horizon, doing a slow turn, then zooming in on the more interesting parts.

Barion stood close enough to look over his shoulder and see what his friend had on the screen.

"Do you see that rock formation, Barion? That is perfect for a trap or an ambush. We could create a monster that lives there and has to be beaten in order to get an additional power? Or life? And the cave over there looks interesting. I wish we had brought the drone. We could have flown it inside to see what it looks like."

"No problem." Barion created another slice in space and stepped through with his arm slung around Jon's waist. The zombie never stopped filming, completely trusting Barion to keep him safe. It was such a heady feeling that Barion's knees went weak. They stood just inside the cave, looking at a vast chamber with the ceiling so high that they couldn't see it. Somewhere had to be a hole because pale light was filtering to the ground, giving the area an eerie feeling.

"I could totally see some monster jumping out of nowhere. This is great!" Jon was taking a few steps forward, his left hand, which wasn't holding the camera, grabbing Barion's right wrist. He followed his friend willingly, as eager as Jon to see as much as possible from the cave. The walls were a pale green with red lines weaving around in a wild pattern. In some places the stone looked as if it had exploded from the inside, and in others as if it had been molten then solidified again. It was totally normal for a hell dimension but still an awesome sight.

Barion had an idea. "How about we make it that the lines in the stone are alive? Something snake-like. Everybody is afraid of snakes. And when you enter the cave, they start following you inside the walls."

"Uhh, creepy, I like it." Jon put the camera down. "Do you think we should build in a twist here? Some secret level? Like when you don't kill the snakes but help the baby snake get out of its stone egg, you get an extra power that allows you to transcend one or two other levels? Or you get a snake to fight at your side in the final boss fight? But the player doesn't know it until they reach the final level?"

"What a great idea! I love the way your mind works, Jon. And if it's not obvious what you get from the secret level, people will wonder about it forever! Well, or at least until they reach the final one."

They both looked around, and Barion was almost sure he could see the red veins moving. *Demon Wars* was going to be a killer game.

"I can practically see it," Jon mused. He had switched off the camera. "The fights taking place in here. We have to give those snakes our all. I don't want them to look generic or anything. Their skin should have a stony quality but be fluid, like lava. What do you think?"

Barion grinned. "Sounds great. And as for the other monsters, I can show you what runs around in the hostile dimensions."

"Well, I've seen the giant sunflowers that shoot their seeds at everybody walking by." Jon shuddered. "That's an image I could have done without. The demon they hit was in so much pain."

"It didn't last long. Besides, Cousin Augias is a drama queen. Yes, the seeds are poisonous and the spelt is acidic, but we heal pretty fast from it. And he was an idiot to charge right into the field. I mean, who does such a thing?" Barion had little pity for his insufferable cousin twice removed.

"They gave us the idea for the poppy and cornflower field, which I still think is as genius as it is devious." Jon's expression was that of a man after a job well done.

Barion chuckled because the poppy and cornflower field was good, and he would bet it could become a hit in the game. The flowers only released their deadly gas when the players ran into the field. If they simply walked — which would have to be a conscious effort on their part because of the three gigantic crabs guarding the field and trying to kill the characters — nothing happened. And the crabs wouldn't enter the field, which the players wouldn't know. Barion had to admit creating a game was incredible fun.

Jon stepped closer to him. "I think I've gotten enough inspiration. Let's go back home?"

Barion nodded. Time was passing differently here anyway and staying too long meant they could miss an entire week on Earth. He did the slicing and they stepped into Jon's living room.

After they had put away the backpack and gotten something to drink, Barion looked at the clock. They had been gone for almost the entire day. It was now five in the afternoon. Jon leaned back on the couch, his eyes fixed on Barion.

"This was so much fun, Barion. Thank you. I have one question, though."

"Fire away."

"Why didn't you take me to a dimension that's populated?"

"Two words. Sunflower seeds."

"Surely there are places that are safe?" Jon cocked an eyebrow.

"Well, 'safe' is a flexible term, as you probably know. What you deem safe and what your Grann views as safe are very different things, aren't they?"

Jon nodded with a shudder. Barion kept talking. "It's my solemn duty that no harm comes to you on our little trips. Protecting you from *potentially* hostile landscape is much easier than defending you against rats the size of bungalows." Barion shook his head. "They have spiked tails. Very nasty."

Jon sat up straighter. "Rats with spiked tails? Can you show them to me?"

"Please, of course I can show them to you. Here, where it's safe. I'm not going to take you to where they live."

"That's fine for me. I have no intention of meeting one eye to eye." Jon shuddered. "I don't even like the rats we get here. But isn't there a dimension you could take me to where it's nice? You mentioned something about 'dungeon dimensions' before."

Barion shrugged. "No. Because first of all, there's a reason humans exist only on Earth. Second, the few dimensions that are harmless are so boring that you'd fall asleep where you're standing, which is their form of defense. Third, yes, I did mention the dungeon dimensions, but after thinking about it, I don't think going there is a good idea. Lastly, the demon wars didn't and can't happen in dull scenery. Where's the fun if the environment isn't trying to kill you while you're fighting against other players?"

"I see your point," Jon agreed. He didn't seem to be too upset, for which Barion was grateful. He found he couldn't stand seeing Jon disappointed. "I hope this was enough input to create all our levels."

What he could stand very well was teasing Jon. "You're not happy with our little trip?" Barion pushed his lower lip forward, trying to make it tremble at the same time. Jon just rolled his eyes.

"While I do find your attempt at channeling Sammy quite hilarious, you still have a long way to go. And I *loved* our trip—but more because of the company and less because of the scenery, which was great and inspiring."

Barion's heart made a suspicious thumping motion. Before he could even start to dissect what had just happened with this important organ hidden deep in his chest, *Don't Pay the Ferryman* started blaring. Jon sighed and took out his phone.

"Yes, Grann?"

Chapter Eleven

"*Enbesil yo!* I should come to Beaconville and drag you back home on your ear!" Grann was furious and had no problem showing it. It was probably the reason she always seemed to be so well-adjusted. Negative feelings didn't get a chance to fester. "It's bad enough you're gallivanting around the globe with your *demontre*, but visiting a powerful *mache espirityel* without knowing if she's friend or foe? Not to mention hopping off into another dimension just to worry your poor old gran into an early grave!"

As usual, Jon didn't comment on the 'poor, old gran' or the fact there was no grave for Grann because she had been there, done that and left it all behind. He did ask about the *mache espirityel*, though.

"You know Waaseyaa?"

Grann huffed. "Of course I do. How many times do I have to tell you? The world of *majik*, it's small when it comes to the real power. You're lucky she isn't an enemy."

"She's Barion's friend," Jon defended the maker of the most delicious pancakes he had ever tasted. He wouldn't mention it to Grann because he was sure good food wasn't a plausible reason to get himself in danger. He needn't have bothered.

"You tasted her *krep*, didn't you?" Grann gave him no chance to answer. "I swear that woman needs to stop enchanting everybody with her damn food!"

"The pancakes are magical?" Jon stared at Barion with wide eyes. His demon friend had obviously heard most of the conversation, thanks to his supernatural hearing, and was now shrugging. *Not enough to be harmful*, he was whispering.

"Of course they are, *enbesil*. All food is magic. I told you that!"

"I thought you meant it in a metaphorical way," Jon said meekly. And he'd thought he'd gotten good at deciphering Grann's words.

"If it's cooked by people, then yes, but if it's a magical person doing the cooking? *Majik* is transcendent, and it always diffuses. Why do you think family gatherings always center around food?"

Grann started mumbling some colorful curses in Creole. Some of the words Jon had never heard and tried to memorize so he could look them up later. *Simply for scientific purposes, of course.* He waited for her to end her rant, which took another five minutes, during which he scribbled the words he wanted to research on a piece of paper Barion had handed him upon request. Finally, Grann was back to talking directly to him.

"No more stupid trips, do you hear me, Jon? No visits to people of *majik* or to a *dimansyon lanfe*. I can't protect you when you're in one of those."

The true worry in her voice kept Jon from saying something snappy about him being able to take care of himself.

"Thank you, Grann, for worrying about me. I love you."

Another curse burned between his ears, then, "I love you, too, *enbesil*." She ended the call.

"That was less of an explosion than I thought." Barion was leaning back on what had become his side of the sofa. Jon pinched the bridge of his nose.

"It was a last warning. We have to lay off the trips for the next few weeks or she *will* be here to drag me back to New Orleans."

"On your ears?"

"It's not funny. She's going to do it, definitely."

"Surely not all the way?"

Jon gave Barion a look. The demon held up his hands. "Fine. You know her better than me. I tell you what. We have enough material to create most of the levels that we wanted to concentrate on, anyway. If we need further inspiration, we can always watch some of the demon wars. And we have already decided to not do the trip to the dungeon dimension, where my father keeps the evil demons. It's for the better, because should my father get wind of it, he'd probably drag me around by my ears as well."

Jon couldn't help but smile. He liked Barion *so* much. "Excellent thinking. Why don't we decide what we want for dinner before we start working?"

"I'm with you. How about *tapas* from Spain? Great food, many choices, small portions, so we can try a lot."

"And I'm sold. You get the *tapas*, and I'll prepare plates and the computers."

It was their usual routine, and Jon couldn't have been happier to have a routine with somebody else, with a friend. Barion bowed.

"*Sí*. And don't forget we have a date later." He winked before he left through the slice in space he had made. Jon closed his eyes.

How could he forget what had become the highlight of each of his days? He couldn't believe his libido had finally woken up and with such force. It was as if Barion was the spark to the dried-up undergrowth his sexual needs had been since his death and subsequent resurrection. Deciding this was something he had to examine more closely when the source of his newfound drive wasn't about to come back any minute, Jon started gathering plates and switching on the computers.

* * * *

It had been a long night full of hard work with a pleasurable end they had both highly deserved. Jon was still half asleep when he realized somebody was at his front door, alternately knocking and ringing the bell. With what could only be described as a zombie shuffle, Jon reached it. After some fumbling with the door lock — technically, there was no need for him to take this security measure because anybody attacking a zombie in his sleep deserved what they had coming, not to mention that encroaching on demon territory was the best and quickest way to commit suicide, not the most painless, but surely the most eventful way to leave the earthly realm — he managed to wrestle the door into submission. Sammy was waiting on the other side with two cups of delicious-smelling coffee and a tray of steaming mini apple pies in his hands. Enough of Jon's brain cells fired up to order his hands to open the door wide, not wanting to risk the goods to vanish again. Sammy stepped inside with a broad smile on his face.

"Good morning, Jon!"

"Good morning, Sammy. It's nice to see you." Jon glanced at the watch on the oven in his kitchen. He could just make it out from where he was standing. "It's already eight o'clock. Aren't you in the shop today?"

"Oh, I will be. Dre is covering for me because I wanted to see how my favorite tenant is doing."

"I'm your only tenant."

"And I couldn't wish for a better one."

Jon sighed, knowing there was no winning against Sammy's kindness. The man ought to wear a license for it. "Let me get plates for the pies. Did Mavis and Maribel make them?"

"Yes. They brought them over and told me to tell you they were made with all their love."

Remembering what he had learned the other day about *majik* and food, Jon eyed the pies with some suspicion. Then a thick waft of the perfect aroma — apples, sugar and *just* the right amount of cinnamon — hit his nose and he forgot all about the potential danger the food might pose. Nothing that delicious could be dangerous, now, could it? They both sat down on the kitchen counter, each with a plate full of pie and their beverage. Sammy had brought Jon's favorite, hazelnut latte with extra milk foam. It made what Jon knew would be coming easier to put up with.

"Sooo, you and Barion?" Sammy had the decency to not even try for subtlety. He had shown what Barion considered remarkable restraint the last few weeks, only a comment here or there during the book club meetings—which Barion hadn't attended, and Jon had been woefully unprepared for because working on *Demon Wars* took up all of his time—and now his friend and landlord had obviously reached the end of his patience.

"Yes, me and Barion. We're friends."

Sammy didn't comment. He simply stared at Jon over the rim of his coffee mug. Jon tried to resist as long as possible but finally gave in when a hint of wetness glazed the soulful look. Sammy was a master not to be trifled with. And Jon had to admit he wanted to talk about him and Barion, just to get some clarity and hear his own thoughts spoken out loud.

"We get along great. We have so much in common and now we're working on this video game, which is going to be great. I can feel it in my bones, and with him, I don't feel shy or awkward at all. It's so nice."

"Mm-hmm."

"He's a great guy. I even like touching him, probably because he's so much hotter than any human could ever be, and when we're together he's mostly in his demon form, so there's no mistaking him for a mortal."

"That's good."

"We went to a tiny diner yesterday to have the most delicious pancakes I've ever tasted before he took me to a hell dimension because we needed inspiration for the different levels of our game."

"Oh."

"What, oh?"

"Barion took you to Waaseyaa. That's an honor you can be proud of. It shows he's as invested in you as you are in him." Sammy was sipping from his cup, a knowing look in his eyes.

Jon didn't want to acknowledge that look for what it was. If he were honest with himself, he was too afraid of the implications. "I told you we're good friends and that we get along great. I've never met anybody whose interests are so similar to mine."

"Before Barion, you'd never met anybody apart from the members of the book club." The statement was made in a dry tone, which didn't make it any less true.

"Then you should be proud of me. I'm meeting lots of new people, thanks to Barion. Although Grann doesn't approve."

"She doesn't like Barion?" The hint of defensiveness in Sammy's tone spoke volumes about how deeply he had already absorbed his brother-in-law into his family.

"It's not that she doesn't like him, per se. She doesn't know him. It's just that she's not overly fond of me hanging around *demontres*, as she calls them, and Barion taking me all over the world and into other dimensions hasn't exactly endeared him to her. She always worries about me."

"It's what family does — worry and love." Sammy smiled softly, with a hint of sadness, and so much love of his own that Jon suddenly understood why everybody, especially paranormal creatures, was drawn to him. He may have been only human before he became Dre's mate, but the love he carried in his heart was a magic more powerful than any other Jon had ever seen. It shone like a beacon, and its warmth gave Jon the courage to ask the question he had been trying to ignore all this time.

"Do you think I could be falling in love?"

The smile became blinding. "Absolutely. It's a beautiful thing to watch."

"But ..." Jon hesitated, gathered all his strength. "Barion is still looking for his mate."

"Has he mentioned it in the weeks you have spent together?"

Now that Jon thought about it. "Not since the very beginning. We've been busy most of the time."

"Then it's safe to say he's not looking as actively at the moment as he had been before he met you. Why don't you enjoy what the two of you have and maybe explore it a bit further?"

"And what do I do once he finds his mate?" Jon realized that was the heart of the matter, the thing he feared the most. What he had with Barion was wonderful, and he didn't want to risk it for anything.

Sammy sighed deeply. "Then you get your heart broken."

"Uhm, that's accurate and entirely *not* what I wanted to hear." Jon felt safe enough with Sammy to admit that.

"It's the truth, broken down to its simplest form. It doesn't cover all the joy you might experience if you dare the jump off the cliff. It doesn't show you all the wonderful things you and Barion could see and do, are already seeing and doing. It doesn't speak of what it would do to you personally to come out of your shell and find trust and love in another being who's not related or your landlord." Sammy grinned. "I don't like the truth in its simplest form. It always misses out on the potential greatness taking high risks promises."

"It's easy for you to talk. Your high risk has given you the ultimate reward." Jon wasn't bitter. He didn't begrudge Sammy his happiness, not in the least. He just couldn't see the same happening for him.

"And I was petrified to take the leap." Sammy bit into an apple pie and moaned in a way Jon was sure should be restricted to the bedroom. It did encourage him to take his own bite, though, and he wasn't ashamed to copy Sammy's sounds of appreciation.

"What made you do it?" Jon had seen what had happened between Dre and Sammy, but he had been an onlooker, thanks to his seclusive ways.

"It was a mixture of being tired of being afraid, of not wanting to postpone the inevitable anymore and of Barion telling Dre and me what utter morons we were."

"Sounds exactly like something Barion would be doing," Jon said with a fond smile.

"And he was right. That demon wouldn't be able to keep his library in order if his life depended on it, but for all his flippantness, he can be surprisingly insightful."

Jon sighed. "I hear you. It's just that you and Dre at least had a hint that you might be mates because of your scent. Barion hasn't mentioned such a thing to me. That I smell good to him, I mean."

Sammy furrowed his brows. "We did have that. But do you know if zombies have a smell at all? I remember Declan and Troy saying something about you not having a scent, which drove them crazy in the beginning."

Jon remembered those first days when the two alpha werewolves had joined their book club and wouldn't stop sniffing him in the hope of getting a scent signature from him. Emilia had been equally bothered but had been too polite to show it openly until Amber had provided the solution. One evening, she had brought a selection of organic soaps that a friend of her made and ordered the three predators to agree on a flavor, which had led to a week-long debate about lavender-lemon versus apple-cinnamon, a discussion Jon hadn't been allowed to join. When they had finally decided that lavender-lemon was better all year-round — versus apple-cinnamon being more of a fall-winter fragrance — Amber had gifted Jon an entire basket of soap bars with the order to use it every day. Declan, Troy and Emilia were satisfied because Jon now had a scent they could associate with him, and he got his soap for free. It was a win-win all around. And when the three wanted to spice things up in the fall, they would give him the apple-cinnamon soap.

"I think it has to do with me being gifted by Papa Legba. I mean, normal zombies stink to high heaven because of all the rotting flesh."

They both shuddered. Sammy cocked his head. "I'm wondering why you haven't retained your scent from before you died." His tone was carefully neutral, telling Jon they could steer away from the topic anytime he wanted if it got too uncomfortable for him. Sammy was such a dear. Strangely, ever since he had started hanging out with Barion, his undead status didn't bother him as much, and he realized he was able to think about his past without wanting to cry, shout or bang his head against the nearest wall.

"I don't know, and to be honest, I did think about it before. I could have asked Grann, but I was too chicken. She and the family were meddling enough as it was without me giving the slightest hint that I might want to find my forever person. I don't even know if zombies have such a thing as a mate."

"The *Walking Dead* kind surely do not." Sammy took another sip of his coffee, and his skin was a bit pale. The man might be cool as a cucumber when it came to real life paranormals and all the gory things they could throw at you, but he absolutely hated films with zombies in them. Jon didn't take it personally. Most of them were terrifying, which, he knew, was the whole reason they were made and watched. Still... He would never understand some people. "But you're not that kind of zombie. You're a gift, a miracle. You should have a mate. Anything else would be unfair."

Sammy said the words with a determination that Jon had learned to fear. His friend had made a decision.

"It's fine, Sammy. I'm not sure I'm ready for a mate yet."

"Oh, you *so* are. Everybody is the moment they meet their mate...when they're adults." Sammy's brow furrowed. "I'm going to start researching zombies and mates. Or you could ask your Grann."

"Uh, no, I think I'll pass. One thing at a time with her. She still needs to get used to Barion."

"I understand." Sammy smiled broadly.

"You really don't have to trouble yourself for me." Jon wasn't sure if he wanted Sammy to find out anything about the mates of zombies. *What if it's something horrible?*

"Oh, it's no trouble at all. You're my friend!" Sammy looked so happy that Jon didn't have it in him to outright forbid him his research.

"Well, then, thank you, I guess."

"You're so welcome! And while I'm looking, you can think about taking a leap with Barion. He's a great guy, and I'm sure you can talk to him about anything. It would be a great learning experience for you both."

Sammy got up, stuffing the last piece of apple pie into his mouth. "I have to go. Dre wants to talk to

Barion before he comes here. When did you want to meet today?"

Realizing he and Barion had been set up, Jon sighed. "It was late yesterday. He's coming for lunch."

"Wonderful. I'm off. Have a nice day. I'll tell you once I find something out." Sammy was through the door before Jon had a chance to say anything else. He stared at the empty plates on his kitchen counter, wondering where his life was headed. As much as he had enjoyed the security his years reclused in the basement had brought him, he had to admit it was more fun now. Perhaps it was time to take that leap. And perhaps he could cheat a little and use a ladder to get down the cliff.

* * * *

Barion was dusting his stag head with the diamonds when Dre popped into his home.

"Brother, what a pleasant surprise."

Dre made a face. "You know, you could try to sound a bit less sarcastic and a good deal happier about your older brother visiting you."

"I could. And you'd know I'd be lying, which would make you say I should be a little more honest. The outcome would be the same...us arguing."

"Hmm. Sounds right. Okay, forget about the happy."

Barion had no intention of letting his brother have the last word. "Plus, I just *know* you're going to pester me about something, most probably Jon. Am I right?"

Dre grumbled something, the red of his scales intensifying, a sure sign he was nearing the end of his

short line of patience. "I'm not just here because of Jon."
His brother sounded defiant. Barion lifted a brow.

"I wanted to tell you that your idea worked. Milo
will be working for Quirion starting next week. He
accepted the raise once he saw how big Quirion's
library is and after our brother talked to him nonstop
for an hour, explaining all his duties to him, along with
all the things Quirion absolutely hates. Afterward, Milo
told me he wanted fifteen percent more." Dre grinned
so broadly that his fangs were clearly visible. His
brother was proud of himself and rightfully so.

"Letting Quirion do the introductions and the job
interview was a genius move, if I do say so myself. Milo
was suspicious when we first told him how much he
would be paid, but now he knows it's not enough." Dre
was laughing out loud and Barion joined him, because
he could just see it in front of his inner eye—his oldest
brother talking Milo into submission.

"That's wonderful news. And I'm glad I could help."

Dre clapped him on the back. "You were great. Now
let's talk about Jon."

Barion groaned, knowing there was no way out of it.
He and Jon would meet for lunch, which was in two
hours. There was enough time for his brother to pester
him.

"What's there to talk about? He's great. We get along
splendidly. We're friends and business partners."

"You took him to Waaseyaa."

"How do you know? Sammy!"

"My beloved mate had breakfast with Jon this
morning, yes."

"We were going on an excursion to a hell
dimension—you know, the one that's in transit at the
moment?—for the game we're developing. It was a

business trip and I wanted us to have a good meal before we started working."

Dre lifted a brow.

"Waaseyaa's pancakes are the best."

"That's not the topic here, Barion."

"Then what is?"

"Don't act dumber than you are."

"Fine. Jon and I are more than friends…probably. I think so. I really like him and being with him is as easy as breathing. Satisfied?"

"Not yet." Dre sat down on one of the chairs standing around. "What are your intentions?"

"Huh? What are you? Jon's chaperone?"

"Would you rather have this talk with Sammy? Or Mavis and Maribel?"

Barion gulped. "I see your point. I'm not sure what my intentions are. We're having fun. Everything's going great. I don't want to rock the boat too much."

"But you like him?"

"A lot." Barion's shoulders slumped. "But I'm also still looking for my mate."

"And Jon can't be it, because?"

"No scent. I know that's not a guarantee with demons, but as you well know, Jon has no scent at all. I'm not even sure if zombies do get mates. I'm certainly not asking him."

"Why not?"

"Because I don't want to hurt him!"

Dre started tipping his chin with one of his claws, no doubt trying to look dignified or some shit when in truth he was just being ridiculous.

"What exactly keeps you from getting more serious with Jon?"

"First of all, who said it's serious at all?"

Dre just lifted one brow, stopping with the annoying chin-tapping to do so. A multi-tasker his brother was not. Barion hissed.

"Fine, it's more serious than I thought it could get."

"Good insight. Now, what keeps you from exploring it further?"

Barion's shoulders slumped. "As I said, I'm still looking for my mate. I could find him tomorrow."

"Or in a hundred years…while Jon is here *now*. Talk to him, be honest, see what he thinks."

"And if he thinks I'm crazy?" Barion couldn't bear even thinking about being rejected by Jon.

Dre shrugged. "Then you won't be talking to each other for at least a week, after which you will start resuming your friendship in a horribly awkward way that will have everybody watching you cringe in vicarious embarrassment then things will slowly get back to normal. Easy-peasy."

"Geez, brother, remind me to never ask you for a pep talk when I really need it."

"Hey, I'm doing my best!"

"You could definitely do with more practice."

Dre pouted. "What are you going to do?"

"There's no chance you're going to let this go, is there?"

"Not before something has happened."

"Tell Sammy he's a pain in the ass."

"Tell him yourself, and don't pin this on him. I want to know as well."

"Fine. I'm going to talk to Jon. Though the protocol, I'm going to blame you if this goes south, understood? Because I don't see why I should shake up a situation that's working so well."

"Understood. Just do it."

Barion showed his brother his tongue, which led to an argument with a small scuffle. The good news was that Barion was able to relieve a lot of nervous energy before going to see Jon.

Chapter Twelve

When Barion appeared in the living room, Jon could immediately tell his friend had had a talk as well. He lifted one brow.

"You talked to Dre?"

"You talked to Sammy?"

They both nodded with a sigh.

"Does this mean we have to talk to each other now?" Jon tried to gauge Barion's mood. The huge demon lifted one shoulder. *Not helpful.*

"We talk to each other all the time." Now Barion winked, the usual mischief shining in his eyes. "And we can absolutely postpone 'the talk' until after we've shown the first avatars to your followers as we promised them."

Jon thought he could live with that.

"*Our* followers. And yes, that's a great idea." He felt some of the anxiety that had been building inside of him since Sammy had left leaving his body. Leave it to Barion to find a way of procrastination that was actually fun. Jon woke his computer while Barion went to the kitchen to put some snacks on plates and get the drinks. It was almost eerie and yet so very soothing how perfect the huge demon fit into the space Jon had once thought was his sanctuary of solitude.

"How is Milo doing in his new job?" Jon had been pleased to hear what solution Barion and Dre had found to help the young man. Despite what he had to done to Sammy, Jon had come to like Milo a great deal.

"He hasn't tried to kill Quirion yet, so I'd say it's going stellar." Barion appeared with a huge plate and two bottles of water.

"Your brother can't be that bad."

"No, he actually isn't. He's worse."

"I don't believe you." Jon sat down in front of his screen while Barion put the plates and drinks between them before doing the same.

"We're talking about a demon who, during the Middle Ages, made it his job to check out all the books copied in the monasteries he could get his hands on, then haunting the poor souls who had made spelling mistakes so they wouldn't make them again in the future. Needless to say, if you deprive humans of sleep, they make even more mistakes. Our father was distracted back then by another demon who—uh, did questionable things—which allowed Quirion to let his inner teacher free, and you don't want to know how many of those monasteries were exorcised, to no avail."

"You're yanking my chain." Jon stared accusingly at Barion. "First, what kind of demonic haunting has ever been about spelling mistakes or books? And second, nobody can read that many books in such a comparatively short time."

Barion shrugged. "First"—he held up his index finger, mimicking Jon perfectly—"I told you Quirion is the least demonic demon I've ever met. Second" — Barion waggled his pinkie — "it *is* possible, and that's all I'm saying about the matter."

Jon remembered the talk about the hidden talents of royal demons and how they were a secret and decided to take the hint. "Do you think Milo is going to ask for a raise?"

"Dre and Sammy hope so."

"Sneaky."

"Yet effective."

They grinned at each other. Jon took a nacho from the plate to nibble on it while he prepared everything for them to go live. The sketches of the first avatars were ready to be uploaded and the music they had selected for it was queued.

"Ready to face the crowd?"

Barion nodded. "So ready."

"We're going live in three, two, one. Hello, friends and fellow gamers. Here are PLM and Big B and today, we're going to share the first avatars for *Demon Wars* with you. Are you ready?"

Sooo ready.

Can't wait.

Show them.

Gimmmmeeee.

On and on it went, the live stream going nuts within seconds. Jon was taken aback by how many people had tuned in and how hyped they were. He and Barion had built anticipation for the avatars and the game by mentioning their progress and even asking their followers for help with tricky decisions like how many additional quests were too many — the answer to that apparently was there couldn't be too many side quests, especially when the way to enter them was well hidden and they led to interesting findings. For *Demon Wars*, Jon and Barion had finally decided that they would have forty-two side quests, because, well, forty-two.

What he hadn't expected was the commitment their followers showed and how involved they got. Word had also apparently gotten around, because the number of people who had subscribed to his channel had more than doubled, which was good for the income he generated through ads.

Barion chuckled into his microphone. "I see you can't wait. Let's get the music playing."

Jon started the drumrolls — cheesy but obviously much appreciated — before he put the sketch of the first avatar on the screen. It was of Augnielle, with some alterations to protect her identity. Skirting the line between reality and fiction had been so much fun, especially since the reality they had to be aware of was what most people would have considered fantasy. Just thinking about it made Jon's head spin in crazy pleasure.

The picture now showed a fierce-looking demoness with light green skin, huge black wings, the pinions doubling as lethal daggers. She wore a leather tunic with runes on it, which made the material stronger than any metal armor. They had given her horns — Barion had chuckled about that for hours and Jon had a feeling if Augnielle ever found out about it, they would be in trouble — and an array of scales in a darker green than the rest of her body on her face, forming a mask around her eyes.

Wow.

Beautiful.

Perfect.

What weapons does she carry?

Do you have an animated version already? I wanna play her!!!

Jon looked at Barion, who grinned. They had a first winner.

"We haven't made a decision about the weapons yet. One idea was to give each avatar their own armory they can access during the game and where they can store weapons. This would make finding new weapons and pimping others a player already has another option in the game. Question is, will we allow the characters to access all their weapons from the beginning or will there be some unlocking process?"

Unlocking process.

All available.

I think available but with the chance to upgrade.

No, I think it's more fun to unlock them with each level, perhaps hide the keys to some weapons in the side quests?

I'd want the weapons from the beginning.

The debate was growing heated, as these things so often did. Jon let it roll for another few seconds, then he pulled up their second avatar, this one modelled after Barion. They had exchanged the deep blue of his scales for a lighter shade, highlighted by silver-white accentuating scales around his shoulders, abs and on his cheekbones.

Oh wow!

He's gorgeous!

Look at those wings. I love the silvery tinge.

A true warrior.

Where can I sign up for the game? I want it now!

Barion chuckled. "Thank you for your kind comments. We very much appreciate them. Sadly, these are the only two avatars already done."

Nooo.

We want more!

Please, give us more!

"But we're working very hard on creating more. The goal is to have ten avatars to choose from, plus an extensive background story for each of them. We've also done research and brainstorming for the landscapes of the different levels and we're looking forward to showing them to you."

Barion was working their audience with practiced ease, building up anticipation without giving away too much. Jon still couldn't believe his friend had never done this kind of thing before. He was such a natural.

"As much fun as it is to talk to you all, we still have a lot of work ahead of us. Have a wonderful week and happy gaming!" Jon cut the stream while the comment section was still buzzing like a hive. The weapon discussion was taking on new steam, while some other gamers had opened a new battlefield about the representation of female warriors in computer games. Jon and Barion hadn't given the topic much thought because they both didn't like the oversexualized avatars some players seemed to prefer, and by sticking close to reality—the one that officially was fiction—oversexualization couldn't happen, because demonesses weren't any different from demons, with the exception of jewelry, which demons were fonder of than their female counterparts but didn't wear in battle because it was impractical. Plus, losing your favorite necklace to a careless sweep of a claw was frustrating as all hell. With a last glance at the comments section, showing him that their female avatar was very well received by the feminist part of the gamers, Jon shut his PC down. He got up from his seat and stretched, letting his bones pop.

"I'd say this was a success."

"A huge one. I never thought they would like the avatars so much." Barion got up as well, stifling a yawn.

"Why? They're really good, even if I do say so myself."

"I think it's because we had so much fun creating them that I never thought of it as work. And if it didn't require hard work, it can't be any good, can it?"

"That's an adorably old-fashioned way to look at things. I know what you mean, of course, because when I was alive, it was the same. If you didn't have to work and bleed and sweat and curse for it, it was worthless." Jon took the almost-empty plates to bring them into the kitchen. "But think about it, Barion. We did bleed and sweat and curse for it. We just never realized it because it was so much fun at the same time. Remember when we couldn't get the color of the scales around Augnielle's eyes right? I recall a lot of swearing on our part." He winked.

"You're right. That one was a bitch. I'm still not entirely happy with how the design blurs when she moves. It's a good thing we only showed them the sketches and not the animated versions."

"This is just the beginning, Barion. We have time to iron out all the little bugs and quirks."

"I know. I know." Barion carried the water bottles to the kitchen.

They stood there, Jon putting the plates into the dishwasher, Barion placing the bottles in the carrier. The atmosphere between them was changing from the relaxed exhilaration of a successful showing to a more loaded heaviness Jon wasn't sure he liked. What he did know for sure, however, was that they had to get it out in the open. He took a deep breath, readying himself for whatever this conversation was going to bring.

"Talking to Sammy was painful—and kind of an eye-opener."

Barion sighed as if the weight of the world was concentrated on his chest. "So was talking to Dre."

"Well, they're mates for a reason."

"You could say that." Barion snorted. "Dre was right though, in many respects." He closed his eyes for a moment. Then he directed his intense gaze at Jon. "For as long as I can think, I was looking for my mate—hoping, praying, he or she would fall into my lap. I've been searching, dreaming. It was such an integral part of my life, this yearning, that I almost didn't realize when it stopped."

Jon wasn't sure what to make of Barion's words. Hope was warring with guilt about keeping his friend from finding his forever partner.

"It stopped?" Jon wasn't capable of more than that.

Barion nodded. "It did. Shortly after the two of us started hanging out. All of a sudden, I wasn't living in a potential future anymore, but in the here and now. I didn't even realize it until Dre pointed it out to me. Don't get me wrong, I still want to find my mate. But Dre made me see how many things I have missed because I was so fixated on my impossible goal."

"It's not impossible. Look at Dre and Sammy."

"They're meeting was pure chance. If Milo hadn't summoned Dre, my brother would have never set foot in Beaconville." Barion took a step closer to Jon, smiling broadly. "Which makes me believe I will meet my mate the same way. By chance. All the searching I've been doing hasn't helped any, so I've decided to relax and let fate or whoever is in charge do its thing."

Jon licked his lips nervously. He noticed how Barion's eyes followed his tongue, a little red bleeding into them. "What does that mean?"

Barion held out his hand and Jon didn't hesitate to put his own inside the huge palm. The warmth flowing through him was reassuring and so familiar that he could have cried.

"It means, I'm open to whatever *you* are open to. I don't know much about your love life except that it's been a bit of a drought. What are your plans, your dreams?"

Jon did feel a tear forming in his left eye at these words. It was true that they had never spoken much about their love lives, mostly due to them being busy with *Demon Wars* most of the time, but also because Jon had known Barion was looking for his mate. He had also been too preoccupied with his newfound libido and the joy of jerking off together to feel the need for an in-depth discussion. Thanks to Sammy, things had changed.

"I'm not even sure I have plans and dreams. You know, when I was still alive, being gay was something you hid in order not to die. I never got along well with my family and always had more pressing matters to think about than who I might want to hook up with — like staying away from my father's belt." Jon shuddered at the memory. Barion squeezed his fingers in silent support, causing more tears to follow their scout down his cheeks. "When I was woken from the dead, it took me a long time to come to terms with everything, and again I wasn't ready to give my sexuality or the finding of a partner much thought. After I came out to my new family, the Honorés, they showed their support by trying to find me somebody, which meant I was busy refusing whoever they wanted to talk me into." Jon chuckled. "Grann even offered to raise a partner for me."

"Oh."

"Yeah. Oh. I talked her out of it. Funnily enough, my family's meddling in my private life—aka my nonexistent love life—is the reason I came to Beaconville in the first place."

"You were fleeing from them?"

"Kind of. I love them, don't get me wrong. But how was I supposed to find somebody if I didn't have any stirrings and was too busy dodging the good-willed matchmaker attempts from my family? I figured coming here would provide me the distance I needed to get some clarity." Jon sighed. "To be honest, before I met you, I was in danger of becoming a total recluse. Sammy didn't let me slip completely, but I wasn't living either and ergo not coming closer to a solution regarding my love life. Everything the two of us are doing is new and wonderful and a lot more than I've ever done before in my life."

"Hmm." Barion was still holding Jon's hand, stroking it gently. "The way I see it, we have a demon who has realized the importance of relaxing and a zombie who is curious for everything that might happen. The two are also friends—very close ones, I might add—who already know how nice it is to share intimacy with the other. Am I correct so far?"

"Very correct." Jon's breath hitched. He always liked it when Barion took charge and sounded like he knew what he was doing.

"So what's keeping us from exploring whatever there is between us? From having fun as friends?" Barion's tone was telling Jon how out of his depth the demon was. And he was insanely grateful that his friend was taking the lead in this difficult and potentially dangerous conversation, making it possible for Jon to *re*act where he would have dreaded to act. He put his other hand in Barion's palm while looking up at him.

"Nothing. Nothing's keeping us from exploring whatever we want. I mean, we went to a hell dimension together. There are no limits for us!" He winked before he got serious again. "Thank you, Barion."

"What for?"

"For being brave enough to talk to me. You gave me the courage to answer."

"Always, Jon. Always."

Barion lifted Jon's hands and kissed his knuckles. The touch of his lips sent shivers down Jon's spine.

"I think I want to do this very much. Explore." Jon closed his fingers around Barion's hand to drag it down to his lips. The heat emanating from Barion engulfed him like a blanket, made him bold and willing to dive into this new adventure.

Chapter Thirteen

"Are we really going to do this?" Barion looked at Jon, barely able to control himself. His heart was still hammering from the leap of faith he had just taken. Barion had known Jon would have never been cruel to him, but exposing himself hadn't come easy. That his wonderful friend had thanked him for his bravery made Barion feel like the king of the world. For Jon, he would always charge into battle headfirst, which made it even more important to keep a level head now. Barion knew what they had just decided was big for both of them, even if it was for different reasons. He wanted Jon to be absolutely sure.

If Jon changed his mind and said he didn't want to make that final step, that he had reconsidered, Barion would respect his wishes, but he would be *very* disappointed. The zombie was an attractive man, inside and out, one Barion could easily picture himself in bed with. Jon pulled his lips from Barion's hand and lowered his gaze to the floor, then back up to him, the heat in his dark brown eyes burning Barion.

"Yes, I am sure. We've been jerking off together for months, and after what you just said, I assume you feel it as well—the connection we share? I want to deepen it even more." There was a hint of vulnerability in Jon's tone when he admitted to the pull between them.

Barion's breath hitched in sheer excitement. "I do feel it, too. And I'd like nothing more than to act on it."

"Then what are we waiting for?" Jon tightened the grip on Barion's hand, led him toward the bedroom. Barion followed willingly, but was hardly able to control himself. He still didn't understand what it was about Jon that pushed his sexual buttons when he should be looking for his mate instead, but he was also way past caring. Jon was there, he was fun, a good man, a perfect friend, a wonderful business partner and somebody Barion loved spending his time with. Hell, Jon had accompanied him on a trip to a hell dimension without batting an eyelash, putting absolute trust in him. It felt only logical to add skin-on-skin time to their list of activities.

He closed the bedroom door without looking away from Jon, who had let go of his hand and was taking off his T-shirt. Barion gulped audibly when he saw the by-now-familiar skin on display, this time in yet another context they hadn't explored. Barion's cock was already fully up, keenly interested in what was going on. Jon made a step toward him, his hands outstretched.

Barion reacted without thinking, letting his instincts take over. He grabbed Jon and yanked him against his chest, stroking his back in long, slow motions. Jon made a mewling sound at the back of his throat, and he tugged at Barion's shirt.

He helped his lover to get it over his head, then dragged him against his now-naked body again. His scales were coming out, the feel of Jon's skin on them almost pushing Barion over the edge because it was so good. Jon groaned, ghosting his hands over the scales.

"Feels so good. You're so hot."

Barion grinned. He knew Jon meant it as a compliment, though not in regard to his looks but his actual temperature, which was hilarious and so typical for the zombie and the relationship they had. He leaned back a bit to get a good look at Jon's face. His dark curls were tucked behind his ears, his eyes glittering with hunger. Barion couldn't hold back any longer. He lowered his head and found Jon's lips in a first, tentative kiss that turned to lava almost instantly. Jon's taste was like an explosion on Barion's tongue, ripe blackberries and cream, and sun, everything good in the world wrapped up in his zombie — and wasn't Jon supposed to not have a scent or taste? Barion felt the thought flaring up before it winked out under the barrage of feelings he was getting. Who needed to think about technicalities when there were more important things to do?

The kiss deepened even more and Barion felt Jon's hands on the button of his trouser, trying to free his cock. Jon was having problems because Barion was so aroused that the material of his jeans was stretched to capacity. Not wanting to waste time, Barion let one of his claws slide out to take care of the problem. After his jeans slid to the ground in two cleanly cut halves, he did the same to Jon's trousers. His lover didn't protest the destructive way Barion treated his clothing, because he was too busy kissing and stroking and touching every inch he could reach. He seemed to be particularly fond of the patches where Barion's scales were already fully out, and because Barion was an attentive lover, he let his natural body armor come forth in full, which earned him a happy moan and even more frantic touching.

Their underwear was gone in an instant as well, the much softer cloth not offering any resistance to the brutal yank Barion gave it. The tearing sound turned him on even more and he wasted no time laying Jon on his back on the mattress.

For a moment Barion was distracted by the slightly reproachful look of the eleventh doctor staring at him from the pillow next to Jon's head. A quick flick of his wrist took care of that problem, the dark blue of the backside contrasting nicely with Jon's light skin tone.

Jon didn't even seem to notice the minor battle Barion had with the Timelord – and didn't get to see his glorious victory either, which was a shame – because he was scratching his fingernails over Barion's back in his attempt to get their bodies as close together as possible. Barion lowered his upper body until scales met skin again, making them both shudder. They started kissing anew, Jon undulating in a way that had Barion reaching down to pinch the base of his cock or it would have all been over that moment. When he was sure he wouldn't shoot his load immediately and drench Jon in cum, he started tracing his fingers over the zombie's skin, feeling the shudders that went through his body that seemed to race directly into his own cock. Fuck, if simply touching Jon felt this good, what would it be like to be *inside* him? Barion moaned at the thought.

Jon was pushing against his chest, urging him up.

"Can't wait. Need you now." He was panting.

"Need to prepare you first." The two braincells still functioning in his brain forced him to say that. No way would he hurt his friend.

"Lube's in the drawer." Jon wiggled under him to get to said drawer, rubbing his thighs against Barion's cock, which in turn made him leak onto Jon like a broken faucet.

"There you are!" With a triumphant scream, Jon held up a bottle with lube. Barion recognized it as the same brand they had bought together shortly after they had started with their Iron Bull jerk-off sessions. He snatched it from Jon's hands with an impatient growl. The tugging at his back told him his wings were trying to unfurl and that he was now fully demon. They would need the entire bottle to get Jon ready for his cock in this state.

Barion caught Jon staring at his fully engorged cock, the silver markings on it standing out in all their glory. The zombie didn't seem to be intimidated. If anything, he looked hungry. Barion wasn't sure if this was Jon's inexperience saving him from freaking out or if the zombie was secretly a size queen. Either way, Barion was glad his lover wasn't running for the hills when confronted with all he had to offer.

In an attempt to calm himself as well as the scorching situation down a bit, Barion took his time to position Jon more in the middle of the bed, where they would have more room to move. The zombie helped as well as he could, lifting his bottom and placing it on the mattress a few inches closer to the center, keeping this half-wiggle up until they both were satisfied with his placement. Barion grabbed a pillow from the head of the bed and Karen Gillan seemed to be approving of what he was doing—he'd always thought she was the best companion the doctor ever had—and shoved it under Jon's ass. Then he parted the beautiful, perfect globes and bent down to have a taste. Again he was swamped by the taste of sun and cream and blackberries, his senses going into overload, making it almost impossible to think straight.

"Want to draw this out," Barion gasped against Jon's hole, which earned him a moan from the zombie. He lifted his head. "But I can't. You're too delicious."

Jon held the opened bottle of lube out to him. "We can do long and slow another time. Need you *now*." A little surprised, Barion realized he loved it when Jon got all bossy with him.

With trembling fingers, Barion took the lube and squeezed a generous amount onto Jon's hole. At least that had been the plan. He wasn't as in control of his strength as usual and the plastic made a creaking sound, lube pouring out of the cracks and over Barion's fist.

"Oops." Barion stared at his hand, not sure what had happened. A huge glob of translucent gel slowly morphed into a pear-shaped drop at his wrist. It extended downward in slow motion, giving Barion and Jon all the time in the world to react. All they did was stare transfixed at the damn thing until it pulled anchor from Barion's wrist and descended onto Jon's hip with a sound like a large insect crashing against a windshield in full flight. They both winced.

Then Jon laughed—a full belly laugh that dialed the sexual tension down several notches, which was good, because Barion had been too close to losing control, case in point, the smashed lube bottle. He laughed with Jon, because it was funny, the way the lube was dripping down his fist. More drops were joining their brother in his entrepreneurial ways onto Jon's thighs, his hips, his ass, the mattress.

After a few minutes of almost-hysterical giggling, Barion felt he had himself under control again. The almost-painful swelling of his cock had receded a bit, and the urge to shoot his load right *now* because otherwise he would implode had lowered to an insistent hum he could ignore for the moment. Carefully he put the broken bottle away, placing it on the nightstand in a way he hoped would keep most of the remaining lube inside, then he started to massage the generous amounts of lube on his hands into Jon's hole, marveling how the soft flesh yielded to his huge fingers.

Barion tried to retain more of his human form and was relieved when his fingers got a little smaller. He didn't want to overwhelm Jon. Though the way his lover was moaning under him, he didn't think Jon had registered the change in size.

The wrinkled flesh was getting softer with each gentle press Barion administered and soon he was able to slip his first finger in to the hilt. Jon lifted his hips, welcoming Barion in a way that had his balls tingling and his cock hardening back to painful. His inner fire flared, and Barion had to concentrate hard to not let it out. Preparing Jon was so erotic that he knew he could come from the sight of his fingers gliding in and out of Jon's hole alone.

Barion had three of them inside by now, the fourth going in on the next stroke with ease. His zombie was pushing against the fingers, fucking himself with jerking motions while he dug his hands into the sheets, bunching them up until they were a ball of cotton cloth. Jon was as turned on as Barion, and somehow that knowledge made it all even better. Barion started scissoring his fingers, moving them around to stretch his lover enough for his cock. Jon's own shaft was bopping up and down, spraying drops of pre-cum everywhere, the scent driving Barion wild. He withdrew his fingers then gathered part of the excess lube from Jon's legs and belly to get his cock all wet. When his shaft was glistening from the stuff, he smeared some more onto Jon's hole before he aligned the tip with his entrance. Jon's breath hitched audibly, his gaze met that of Barion, all molten want and absolute trust.

"I've got you," Barion promised and pressed in. There was a short moment of resistance, the girth of his cock bigger than his fingers, but then Jon exhaled and Barion sank into a tightness so heavenly that he knew instantly he never wanted to leave. He had to grit his teeth to pace his thrust, slowly probing deeper, withdrawing, moving forward again, repeating the motion until he was snuggling his balls up with the curve of Jon's ass. They both moaned when he bottomed out. Jon lifted his face, silently asking for a kiss and Barion was more than happy to give his lover everything he wanted. He enjoyed the heat surrounding his cock while his taste buds got another generous helping of Jon's unique taste.

After what seemed like an eternity, Jon started moving his hips, urging Barion to get things going. Barion was only too happy to comply. He withdrew about halfway, sank down again, watching the pleasure on Jon's face like it was the most fascinating thing in the world...which it was. They danced together like that for a while, their pace steadily increasing until Barion was slamming into Jon like he had something to prove. He could feel Jon getting close to orgasm, the zombie working his cock frantically. Barion matched his movements, feeling his own release building like a tidal wave.

When it crashed, Barion was lost. The combination of Jon's scent, his beautiful body under Barion, welcoming his demonic form so perfectly, his low moans and drawn-out groans, it all was too much. Something inside Barion's brain fizzled out—later he would argue it was his common sense, which would make Dre break out in peals of laughter—and with it died any and all inhibitions Barion might have still had. He lowered his head and acted purely on instinct, the demon taking charge. Jon was his, his alone, and he would show it to the whole world. His fangs dropped, and his gaze locked on Jon's. The zombie's eyes were hazy, as if he were in a trance. It didn't stop him from exposing his neck to Barion, the submissive gesture triggering the most primal part of the demon. He sank his fangs into the junction of Jon's neck and shoulder, pumping his venom into his lover's veins the same time his cum flooded his ass. Jon screamed in utter bliss, his ass clenching around Barion's shaft, milking him hard while his own seed spurted between their bodies, painting their bellies in splashes of white.

On and on it went, a circle of pure bliss, until Jon's cries were no longer ecstatic. They were full of pain now, and the moment Barion realized what was happening, what he had done, he didn't know if he should panic, rejoice or kick himself for being so inconsiderate and out of control as to bite his sex-partner. He decided to go for joy, mixed with a heavy dose of guilt when Jon started writhing in agony on the mattress.

Now that it was happening, Barion wasn't surprised to realize that Jon was his mate. It wasn't this big light bulb moment some cartoon characters had, more like a very content *of course, what did I think would happen?* They fit so perfectly, who else could it have been? The only thing that annoyed him was how blind he had been to the possibility. Then again, it was perhaps for better. Getting to know Jon as a friend without all the implications of probable matehood hanging over them was preferable to freaking out every time they met. And freaked out he would have, because Barion was demon enough to admit his failings.

Knowing he could do nothing to soothe his mate's pain, yet wanting to, he pulled him into his arms and held him through the spasms while his body adjusted to being a demon's mate.

Jon was confused. One moment he'd been flying so high that he thought he could touch the sky, and the next he'd been dragged into a hell of pure pain and suffering. Now he was standing on a dark plain with the ghostly outlines of a city in the distance, the corpses of long-dead trees providing a suitable background to the overall gloominess of wherever he was.

"I'm sorry. It's just the way things are here." The voice sounded amused and came from close to the ground. Jon turned around and found a black cock standing there. It had an impressive set of spores and the beak promised pain if the wearer were provoked.

"Who are you?" Jon asked, even though he had an inkling. The cock tilted his head to the side.

"You know me." It sounded smug.

"You're Papa Legba."

"*Smart boy.*" *The cock scratched the ground a bit with his left leg. If it was deliberate or just avian habit, Jon couldn't tell and certainly wouldn't ask. He doubted there were worms to be found here, though weren't worms linked to corpses? Could a worm survive here? And if so, did that mean there were such things as zombie worms? Or were all worms magical? And how would they look? Not the usual pinkish orange hue they had on Earth, he was sure. Perhaps they were black worms. Yeah, that sounded about right, and Jon wasn't sure if he was going crazy or if his brain was simply trying to protect him from whatever was happening at the moment.*

"*What am I doing here?*" *That was a much safer question than asking about potentially undead worms and avian habits and dead people, and also the one he was a lot more interested in.*

"*You're being marked as a demon's mate. Traditionally, the mate's mind or spirit, or however you wish to call it, goes to a different place to make the pain more bearable – a smart mechanism, if you ask me, because who would want to spend eternity with the person who gave you the worst pain of your existence while having sex? Humans tend to meet deceased loved ones, telling them goodbye or, in some cases, fuck off. Humans are weird.*" *Papa Legba shook his head, the cockscomb – as black as the feathers – at the top tilting to the side.*

"*And I get to meet you?*"

"*Would you rather talk to your father?*"

"*Good point.*" *Jon shuddered.* "*Since I'm already here, there's something I always wanted to ask you.*"

"*Be my guest.*"

"*Why me? I mean there was a room full of corpses, and you woke me. Why?*"

The cock did look a bit flustered, if poultry could be flustered. Was Papa Legba poultry? Technically the outer form did say something about what was inside. Again, Jon decided not to follow that special train of thought.

"I can take on any form I want. This is just the one I happen to like best. Plus, I thought it would be easier for you to talk to me like that. Not as threatening."

Jon had seen **The Birds** *by Hitchcock. He had never trusted avians since then. "Can you read my mind?"*

"It's not hard. You're pretty obvious." Papa Legba shook his wings. In combination with his spores and the beak, it was way more impressive than what Jon usually associated with poultry, and he already saw himself sitting on a bench while the cocks gathered behind him in the trees.

"So why did you do it? Grann says you always have a greater plan in mind."

"Your Grann is a very wise woman, and I'm honoréd to have her as my priestess." The cock clucked. "Did you get that? 'Honoréd', like in Honoré?"

"Uh, yes, hilarious."

The cock murmured something about casting pearls before swine. Jon waited patiently for Papa Legba to get back to the original question. After some more grumbling, he went on, "I have to admit the greater plan with you was to see what the greater plan was."

"Excuse me," Jon said. "Somehow I just heard I was used as some kind of guinea pig."

"Not exactly as a guinea pig. No, I wouldn't use that term." Papa Legba fluffed his feathers, which made him appear bigger. Because his feathers were also deep black and shiny, he looked a bit like a drowned rat – whose corpse could still bite off Jon's finger. "You have to understand that sometimes I don't see that clearly. I'm not the one who decides fates. That's the Norns' job, weaving and all that shit. It's a bit hard to do with a beak, if you get my meaning? All I sense is importance, but I can't connect it to anything. On that day, when Amede begged me to bring Grann back, I

could feel there was somebody else who needed to wake up. I didn't see why or to what end, but I just knew it was important. And here you are, being marked as the mate of a demon prince. I'd say my hunch was spot on." The cock preened.

Unfortunately, Jon couldn't say much against that. Finding his mate was a dream come true and said mate being Barion, his best friend and business partner? It was perfect.

"I guess I have to thank you for waking me up." He must have sounded sadder than he intended, because suddenly the cock was gone, and he was surrounded by a presence of pure warmth and comfort. The words formed in his mind.

"I'm sorry you had such a hard time. I know how difficult it can be to leave my dominion behind, and I would have never done it for the heck of it. I hope you know that."

Jon closed his eyes and leaned into Papa Legba's embrace, accepting the comfort he was offering. "I know. And I have a mate now, so it was worth it. Thank you."

"You're always welcome."

Jon heard a chuckle. "I think you need to go back now. The marking is done. Have a wonderful eternity, child of mine. I'm proud of you."

The warmth receded, only to be replaced by pure heat, the heat of a demon. Jon slowly opened his eyes and met Barion's red gaze. They stared at each other for some time, Jon not knowing what to say that would properly reflect the gravity of the moment and Barion obviously not faring any better. Finally, the demon opened his mouth.

"Uh, sorry, not sorry?" his friend and mate — yes, his *mate* — offered sheepishly.

Jon grinned, relieved at the immediate drop in tension. Trust Barion to make things right for both of them.

"Apology accepted, not accepted." He slung his arms around Barion's neck. "We're mates. How cool is that?"

"Definitely cooler than just being friends."

"And we didn't have to go through the whole 'are we, are we not, should we do it, should we not' that Dre and Sammy endured."

Barion pressed a kiss to Jon's forehead. "Yeah, it was agonizing to watch. I'm so glad we got our swift kick in the butt without anybody thinking we could be mates."

"You really had no idea?"

"Not the slightest." Barion leaned down to press a kiss to Jon's forehead. "I just thought having sex with my best friend could turn out to be either great or a complete disaster. I guess 'great' won the day."

"Definitely." Jon felt a stupid smile tugging on his lips. "And I thought zombies didn't get mates at all. I'm so happy."

"Me too, babes, me too." Barion leaned down to catch Jon's lips, his fire racing through Jon the moment skin met skin, promising him he would never be cold again. Jon slung his arms around Barion's neck, accepting his mate and everything he had to offer, giving himself wholly in return.

* * * *

The next morning, Jon was sitting at the kitchen counter, watching Barion make coffee and marveling at the strange yet wonderful turn his life had taken all of a sudden. He looked down at his naked chest, which was covered in demonic runes, proclaiming for the world to see who he belonged to. Just half an hour before, while still in bed, Barion had explained what all the wriggles and loops meant. *Jon, mate of Barion, Demon Prince, son of Alerion, Demon King*. There were other relations mentioned—Barion's mother, as well as Dre and Quirion, and a beautiful little loop around his navel that resembled a butterfly represented Sammy. Having this connection to his landlord and friend made Jon even happier than he already was, especially when Barion explained to him that Dre and Sammy, along with the rest of Barion's family, would—with time—get additional demonic runes to mark the growth of their line as well.

Jon was all for growth, especially in certain parts of his mate's—*mate's*—anatomy. It made shivers run down his spine and his cock plump. Barion turned to him with a knowing smirk, no doubt having sensed the naughty direction Jon's thoughts had taken. The gleam in his eyes said he was very much on board with whatever Jon wanted to do. Before either of them could act on the tension rising between them, *Don't Pay the Ferryman* blared from his cell. Jon sighed.

"It's Grann. I guess we can be grateful she didn't call the moment I was marked." He reached for his phone and took the call. "Hello, Grann."

"I don't know if I should congratulate you or chew you out for your carelessness, *enbesil*. Sleeping with a demon for *fun*?" Jon cringed then saw Barion trying to suppress a chuckle. The man was insufferable.

"Your *demontre*, he's listening, isn't he? Put me on speaker." Jon obliged, shooting Barion a warning glare. The demon just smiled.

"Hello, Mrs. Honoré. It's a pleasure to finally meet you, even if it's just over the phone. I'm Barion, third son of Alerion, the king of all demons. Jon has told me so many good things about you already."

"Throwing your titles around won't save you, young man, nor will your sweet talking, though you can keep going. It warms an old woman's heart to be appreciated."

Jon rolled his eyes. Barion bowed with a flourish, apparently forgetting that Grann couldn't see him. "Well, I know you took Jon under your wing after he came back from the dead, and I'm eternally grateful for it because it made finding him possible for me." If Barion was laying it on any thicker, he would slip on his own trail of slime.

"*Wi*, you found him—by chance, I heard. So you weren't serious about my grandson?" The hint of steel in Grann's voice made Jon snicker. He muffled the sound by slapping his hand over his mouth while Barion shot him a dirty look.

"Quite the contrary, ma'am. I was serious about Jon as my friend, and as friends, we decided to have ourselves a little adventure. Nobody is happier than me how it turned out." Barion winked at Jon.

"Nice save, *demontre*. And I think you can call me Grann, seeing as you're family now. Speaking of which, I'm expecting you here the day after tomorrow. I want to meet and welcome my new grandson in person, and the family wants to get to know him."

Jon groaned inwardly. Getting to know him meant grilling Barion relentlessly until their curiosity was satisfied. He also didn't dare mention his mate—*his* mate! *How freaking cool is that?*—was her senior by several centuries. Just thinking about how much weirder his family constellations had suddenly become—and he hadn't thought there was room for improvement on that front. Ha!—felt somehow wrong and creepy, and he wished his brain would shut up already.

"Of course, Grann. I can't wait to meet Jon's family. We're looking forward to it." Barion clearly didn't know what he was getting into. And Jon wasn't sure what he wanted more, to protect his mate or show him off to his family. The decision was taken from him anyway.

"We'll be there, Grann. Is noon all right?"

"*Wi*, Jon. We can have lunch together."

"Should we bring anything?" Barion was still trying to get himself some brownie points.

"It's fine, Barion. The family will cook." Meaning, they would all be there. Jon didn't comment.

"Wonderful, Grann. See you the day after tomorrow."

"See you." She hung up and Jon slumped in his chair.

"This is going to be a massacre."

"It's your family, *iubit*. I want to meet them. Besides, you're going to have to put up with mine. It's only fair." Barion winked.

"Believe me, it's not fair. Your family basically consists of your two brothers, one of whom I'm already friends with, while the other never leaves his library, and your father, who is, yes, the king of all demons but also pretty nice. That's it. My family consists of everybody of that bloodline who has ever lived and is currently alive. We're talking hundreds of people, all intent on poking their noses where they don't belong. They're going to swamp us."

"Oh, I hadn't thought of that." Barion seemed to consider his options. "You know, we can always go on another tour around the hell dimensions. Now that you're a demon's mate, you should be fine surviving all of them."

"I'm not even going to start thinking about all the things wrong with that sentence."

"It's probably for the better. Sorry... I was panicking." Barion stepped toward him, pulling him into a hug that was mostly comfort and only slightly sexual. Jon snuggled into him.

"It's fine. You have a right to panic. Let's enjoy breakfast then go back to bed?"

"How about we go to bed right now?"

"I have such a smart mate." Jon laughed when Barion hoisted him up in a fireman's carry. He almost didn't realize they were going through a slice in time and space before he was dumped on the mattress. *Why is Matt Smith staring at the sheet?* Jon took the pillow to turn it around, but Barion snatched it from his hands.

"What?"

"I don't like the way he's looking at me. I think he's judgmental."

Jon looked at his mate then at the pillow in his hands. From there, his gaze wandered to the second pillow with Karen Gillan, who was right side up.

"*She* approves," Barion grumbled.

"And Matt Smith doesn't?"

"You should have seen him yesterday!"

Jon held up his hands in surrender. He didn't think this was an argument he was going to win, and besides, he had more important things on his mind—like sexy fun times with his mate. "Do with him whatever you want."

He hoped Matt Smith would forgive him, but a zombie had to have priorities. Jon watched as Barion tossed the pillow on the ground before he blanketed Jon with his huge body. *Yes, priorities.*

Chapter Fourteen

Barion was ready for a little post-coital nap with his gorgeous mate when he heard somebody knocking at the door of the apartment. Jon sighed against his pecs, the soft breeze creating a tingle on Barion's scales.

"I don't want to get up."

The knocking sounded again, more insistent.

"Then don't. Whoever it is will come back later."

The knocking took on a faster pace.

"Are you sure?" Jon buried his face deeper in Barion's scales.

"Absolu" — a rip appeared in thin air and Dre stepped through, Sammy hot on his heels — "tely. They will just invite themselves in," he added drily.

Jon sat up quickly, the blanket fell down to his hips, revealing his glorious torso. Sammy and Dre stared wide-eyed for a moment, then Sammy squealed and threw himself onto the bed to give Jon a hug.

"Ooooh, is this what I think it is?"

Jon looked a bit overwhelmed. His arms had closed around Sammy's back automatically without his usual hesitancy.

"Uh, I don't know what you think it is?"

Dre looked as if he were constipated. Barion knew that look and, sure enough, the lecture ensued. "If I remember correctly, I told you to talk to Jon and see where things would go. I never mentioned biting."

Barion felt his scales heating, which elicited a purring sound from Jon, who was pressed more tightly against Barion's chest by Sammy's weight. Jon's expression of happiness made Dre roll his eyes—*he's such a diva*—and Sammy squealed happily again.

"I admit that I got carried away." Barion was very proud of himself for delivering this line with a straight face.

"Carried away? Making a cake and eating all the dough is being carried away. Biting your sex-partner on your very first encounter is something else entirely! It was the first encounter, wasn't it? Why am I even asking? I need bleach for my brain. My baby brother—"

"Dre, beloved, it's fine." Sammy leaned away from Jon, thus relieving the weight on Barion's chest a bit, to stroke Dre's arm in a soothing manner. "You knew Barion had a sex life."

"But there was never any proof!" Dre wailed.

"Now he's tainted, like...like..."

"Like you?" Barion couldn't resist.

Dre shot him an angry glare. "That's different and you know it."

"How is that diff—?"

"Uhm, I didn't mind getting bitten. In fact, I'm glad Barion did it." Jon *did* sound happy.

"You're saying that now," Sammy muttered with a wink.

"Argh, I can't un-imagine this! My brother and his mate doing I know not what!"

"Oh, I'm pretty sure you know exactly what we did." Barion grinned at his agitated brother.

"Dre, beloved, I think you're overreacting. They're both adults and, more importantly, both happy. Don't you want our brother and our friend to be happy?" Sammy was using the quivering lips. His gorgeous bi-colored eyes were huge. Barion felt placating words forming on the tip of his tongue without conscious effort on his part. Such was the *majik* of seemingly helpless little humans. Dre, experienced mate that he was, beat Barion to it.

"No, *mo grah thu*, of course I wish them both the best, and I'm so happy for them. It's just a shock. I mean, we wanted them to live a bit and now they're mated."

"The best shock *ever!*" Sammy announced while he flung himself on Jon again, trying to include Barion in the hug. It was awkward and so nice.

"And here I thought we would just be checking on Jon and see if you two had that talk we suggested. Seems our advice was spot on, hmm?" His brother now sounded as smug as he had been outraged only a minute ago. Barion was willing to hit him on the head right then and there.

"You were right. There, I said it. But I want to point out, very firmly, that you didn't have the slightest clue *this* was going to happen." He gestured at Jon, who was still hugged fiercely by Sammy who had finally realized his arms were too short to get them both. "So technically, you just got lucky."

"We just got *lucky*? Sammy, have you heard him?"

Sammy was looking up from where he was smothering Jon. "To be honest, Dre, we just thought it would do both of them good to get some before tumbleweeds started invading their piping."

The absolute innocence in Sammy's tone while saying something so shocking made it very clear who the originator was. Barion shot his brother a dirty look. Dre just shrugged, completely unrepentant.

"I was right, wasn't I?"

"Can we please talk about how wonderful it is that Jon is now my brother?" Sammy had let go of Jon and was now bouncing on the mattress like an overexcited child. "By the way, why is Matt Smith on the floor?"

"Long story."

"Barion thinks he's judging him."

Dre picked up the pillow and took a long look at the eleventh doctor. "Well, he does look a bit judgmental in this picture."

"Are you sure?" Sammy leaned forward, almost fell off the bed in his attempt to get the pillow from his mate and was saved by Dre, who simply lifted him up with one hand while holding the pillow up for inspection with the other. "Hmm, I'd say he always looks like that. And why would you think he's judging you? It's Jon's pillow."

Jon groaned. "Don't involve me in this madness. Matt Smith approves of everything I do."

"I like Karen Gillan better." Dre glanced at the redhead who still had a place on the bed.

"See? I told you so." Barion huffed.

"Let me get this straight. You argue about practically everything, but you stick together like glue when it comes to Karen Gillan?" Barion wasn't sure if Jon's expression conveyed more horror or disbelief.

"There are some unalterable principles one has to follow." He tried to sound aloof. When Sammy opened his mouth, no doubt to say something that would shatter Barion's and Dre's reputation forever, he hurried to change the topic. "Anyway, Jon and I are very grateful for your intervention. I still can't believe I didn't even suspect he could be my mate."

"We didn't either, which makes this sooo good." Sammy was standing on his own again, snuggled against Dre with a happy smile on his lips. "When are you going to tell Dad? Uh, can Dre and I be there as well? We could have a family dinner, perhaps get food from Zenobia and go to Milano for dessert. And when do you want to have the great announcement party? Oh my gosh, you have to tell the book club, and there's so much to organize. But don't worry. I'll be there for you. I know how it all works, I still have all the numbers from caterers and florists and I'm sure Maribel and Mavis will want to contribute as well. This is *so* great!"

Sammy was clapping his hands; his cheeks were an adorable shade of red. Barion looked at Jon. His mate seemed stunned and his mouth was hanging open. Perhaps it was all a bit much for one morning. Barion grabbed Jon's shoulders to tug him under his arm, where the zombie settled with a sigh.

"I think we need a little time to get used to this." Barion smiled at Sammy in an attempt to rein him in a bit. "Besides, Jon's Grann called this morning. She's expecting us in New Orleans the day after tomorrow. As Jon explained to me, his family is huge, which means things are going to be exhausting."

"Oh, I get it!" Sammy changed from overexcited puppy to understanding friend within seconds. It was a joy to watch and reminded Barion how much he loved his brother-in-law, no matter what a pest he could be. "You know what? You two enjoy your first day as mates, and Dre and I take care of everything else. We'll inform Dad, Quirion and the book club and tell them you need some time to yourself. Once you're back from New Orleans, we can talk about dates and location and all the rest."

It was such a wonderful offer, exactly what Jon needed if Barion interpreted the sudden complete relaxation in his mate's body right. Jon looked up to Sammy. "Thank you so much. This is all so sudden. I still don't know what to think."

"Then don't think." Sammy made a step toward the bed, took Jon's hands in his, the smile on his lips full of affection. "Spend time with your mate, and get ready for the meeting with your family." He put a finger to his lips. "You're probably not going to get much rest, but who needs that when you have a mate?" Sammy's wink could have been suggestive—he no doubt was aiming for innuendo—if it hadn't been for the genuine excitement in his voice. His brother's mate was too innocent for his own good.

Jon leaned a bit forward, tugging on Barion's arms around his torso, to squeeze Sammy's hand. "I know I don't need rest. Thank you, Sammy, Dre."

"You're welcome." Dre dragged Sammy away from the bed. "Come on, *mo grah thu*. We need to tell the others."

"They're going to be so excited!" Sammy snuggled up to Dre, who was opening a rift for them to step through. "Should we ask Dad to meet us at this wonderful café in Sweden? Somehow I have a hankering for their hot chocolate."

"Whatever you wish, *mo grah thu*."

The rift closed and Barion and Jon were alone again.

"Phew, that was intense." Jon was leaning back against Barion's chest, his dark hair caressing the scales.

"Too much?"

"No. I love Sammy like a brother, and Dre has become a good friend. It's just—" Jon started playing with the fingers on Barion's right hand. "You know, I came to Beaconville to escape my nosy family, to find peace and quiet and time to myself."

"And now you have a mate, another nosy family and no peace and quiet." Barion made sure Jon could hear the amusement in his voice.

"The mate I don't mind at all, quite the contrary. I still can't believe I found you, that we found each other. The nosy family I almost instantly got upon arrival in form of the book club. I still have the suspicion Mavis and Maribel are reporting back to my Grann."

"What makes you think so?" Barion was genuinely interested, as he never had much contact with witches before Dre had met Sammy.

"Well, as my Grann likes to say, the world of *majik* is small and she, as well as Mavis and Maribel, have dropped some hints that they know each other. My Grann also knows Waaseyaa."

"It seems to me your Grann knows a lot of people."

"That she does." Jon sighed. "It's nice to know she's looking out for me, even if it annoys me sometimes."

"Family." Barion started tracing the markings on Jon's torso with his finger. That was so much better than talking about relatives and all the horrors they could bring upon an unsuspecting demon or zombie. Jon was obviously very much on board with getting physical again, because he started squirming against

Barion's body, causing his cock to go from interested to eager within seconds. Well, it was their honeymoon, so to speak, and with Sammy and Dre taking care of his side of the family and the visit to Grann looming on the horizon, they had the day to themselves.

A few eventful hours later, they got up for something to eat. Out of habit, Jon checked his email while Barion was distributing the *Kroppkakor* he had gotten from a restaurant in Smaland — Sammy's mention of hot chocolate from Sweden had given him a hankering for the dish — on two plates.

"Holy ancestors!" Jon's scream had Barion almost dropping the plates on his way to the coffee table in the living room. He narrowly managed to balance the dumplings before they went on a journey downward and hurried over to Jon, putting the food safely down.

"What's wrong, *iubit*? Are you hurt?"

"No, but holy crap on a cracker, look at this!" Jon gestured at his screen where an email was open. It took Barion a moment to realize what he was reading.

"That's from Endless Horizon. *The* Endless Horizon? Please tell me it's what I think it is!" He had grabbed Jon's arm and was shaking it wildly. His wonderful mate reciprocated by digging his fingers into Barion's wrist.

"It's definitely *the* Endless Horizon, one of the biggest gaming companies out there. I've worked with them before, so I can tell this is genuine."

"And they want *Demon Wars*?" Barion was re-reading the mail for the third time.

Dear PLM and Big B,
We are great fans of your channel and have been following the reviews for quite some time – using them ourselves, we

might add. *With greatest interest have we noted your idea for a brand-new computer game. We love the idea, the story building, the way you're planning to create it and let's just say the first two avatars you've introduced are brilliant. We would like to offer our assistance in your endeavor so it may reach the greatest heights possible.*

Please contact us at your earliest convenience,
With best regards,
Jim Dalton and Annabelle Lee
CEOs of Endless Horizon

"Endless Horizon wants *Demon Wars*. How incredible is that?" Jon was vibrating next to him. "What do you think? I mean, we could do this on our own, but having somebody like Endless Horizon backing us? It's a huge chance."

Barion pressed a kiss to Jon's temple. "I'm fine with whatever you want to do. Yes, this is our baby, and doing this on our own is what has brought us together, but having access to the knowhow of such a huge company? It's worth thinking about."

"I think we should definitely talk to them and see how they would want to play this. If we don't like it, we can always back out." Jon's fingers were already hovering above the keyboard.

"Then do it. When do we want to talk to them?"

"How about Friday? It's Monday. We'll be in New Orleans on Wednesday and back Thursday, Friday morning at the latest. And if we can cite a business meeting, we have no reason to extend our stay over the weekend."

"You are such a smart man, my mate." Barion kissed Jon again, this time on the top of his head. The soft dark locks teased his lips, gave him some delicious ideas that had nothing to do with computer games and everything with christening the couch. Having a mate was so much better than he had ever imagined.

Chapter Fifteen

Wednesday came quicker than Jon had ever thought possible, time flying as if it wanted to spite him. He and Barion had been busy having sex in every single possible spot in his apartment — as well as some impossible places — and working on the levels of *Demon Wars* in between. The new physical component to their relationship seemed to fuel their creativity, and work was flowing so easily that Jon almost found it eerie. Now it was time to face the family. Barion's side, as well as the book club, had shown remarkable discipline, respecting their wish for privacy, with only Sammy coming by Tuesday evening to report how happy they all were for them. Jon had no illusions about how things would be at his Grann's.

"You said your Grann lived on Saint Louis Street?" Barion was in his half-demon mode as Jon had silently named it. It was very obvious from his deep blue scales and almost eight feet that he wasn't human, but the wings and horns were still hidden. His demon was so gorgeous that Jon was drooling.

"Yes. Do you think you can get us there?"

"*Iubit*, I can get us anywhere." Barion winked. "I just think I'm going to open the portal at the crossing of Burgundy Street. I know a nice quiet alley there where we can pop up. Since I haven't been to your Grann's yet, I don't want to accidentally destroy something or alarm anybody. It's funny how people can get all worked up about a rift opening in their living room."

"Yeah, very thoughtful of you, taking people's sensitivities into consideration."

"You do realize I know sarcasm when it hits me in the face?"

"One of the things I love about you." Jon lifted his face for a kiss and his incredible mate complied immediately.

"And I love you, my zombie surprise."

The first time they had said the L-word, it had felt strange, like an unknown taste in his mouth. Jon thought it was because he had never deemed it possible that he would have love, not to mention a mate. They had both practiced and now the declaration flowed easily from their lips, feeling so right that it almost hurt.

"Ready to go?"

Jon took a deep breath. "As ready as I'll ever be."

Barion lifted his hand, did the familiar slicing that took them from a moderately tempered spring day in Beaconville to the humid heat that was New Orleans. The alley he had mentioned was more of a deadlock, smelling of everything that should never be left out in this heat for any amount of time. It was also so narrow that Jon wasn't even sure if it could be called an alley. *More like a passage or a squeeze way. Is there such a term as 'squeeze way'? There definitely should be.* And he was panicking because his brain was going all directions in a desperate attempt to escape from what was coming.

"Hey, *iubit*, it's going to be fine. This is your family. Remember that they love you."

"I know, and I love them. I just want them to love you as much, and I'm terrified they won't, even though there's no reason and—"

"Shhh, it's fine. Let's go." Barion pulled him under his arm before he started to leave the squeeze way. *Yep, a word. A good word.* The walk along Burgundy Street to the crossing with Saint Louis Street was short, shorter than Jon remembered it to be. They went past the familiar beautiful houses with their brick walls and wrought-iron balconies filled with flowers of all colors until they reached his Grann's house, one of the oldest in the area. The bricks were a little darker, the shutters of the floor-length windows painted in an intricate pattern of soft lilac, pastel green and a vibrant yellow. The wrought iron wrapped around balcony on both stories and was overgrown with ivy and passionflowers, and the porch was painted pink and flanked by two golden raintrees. It was a tranquil sight in the hubbub of the French Quarter, at least until they entered through the wooden gate with the whittled cocks guarding it from their perch on the poles. Once they set foot on the dirty brown gravel—Grann had never seen the appeal of white gravel, saying she distrusted things that pretended to be pure, even though Jon suspected her reasons were of a more practical nature concerning cleaning costs, but he wasn't dumb enough to say that out loud—all hell broke loose. All of a sudden, the air was filled with the ghostly apparitions of ancestors who were swarming them like bees defending their nest, cries of welcome mixed with the first questions, all merging to one big wall of sound where only single words were audible.

*Demontre...pwalkom...*welcome...*te sonje ou...*missed you...what are your intentions...*majik...dezod...* chaos...*enkyetid...*unseen...*danje...*danger...

"That's enough!" Grann stepped onto the porch, wearing a beautiful scarlet red dress with huge flowers printed on it in white and blue. The chattering stopped and the ancestors were hanging in the air like puffs of smoke. Jon looked at Barion, who didn't seem to be fazed at all. His mate was so confident, and why shouldn't he be? There was practically nothing that could really hurt a demon. Barion tugged Jon a little closer to his side to comfort him before letting go of him so he could greet his Grann.

"Grann." Jon went to her, grabbing Barion's hand to drag him along. No way was he leaving his mate alone. No way was he walking up there alone. They were one.

Grann smiled broadly, her eyes full of warmth as she opened her arms. Jon sank into the hug, the familiar scents of herbs and *majik* and death surrounding him, soothing him. Grann opened the circle of her arms on one side, tugging Barion in as well, not an easy feat for a woman of only four foot nine — there had to be magic involved, Jon was sure of it — and she was greeting them with soft words.

"Welcome home, *cherie*, and welcome to the family, Barion."

"Thank you, Grann." Jon could feel Barion's smile in his words.

"It's good to be back." Jon leaned his head back a little to look at Grann's face. He thought he saw a shadow in her usually bright eyes, there and gone again so fast that he was sure he had only imagined it.

"Good enough to stay, *cherie*?" Grann winked when the chorus of ancestors started anew, chattering away about wonderful houses in the area, the perfect places for a zombie and his demon mate to live.

"I'm afraid not, Grann. But we're going to visit you regularly. Thanks to Barion, there's no need to book a flight or drive a car."

"The joys of being mated to a *demontre*. Let's go inside. Barion needs to be introduced." At those words, the driveway was suddenly empty. The ancestors had all gone into the house to look at the food and criticize it. One of the joys of being an ancestor was that they got to tell their offspring how bad they were at cooking.

Jon and Barion followed Grann into the generous hall with the dark blue tiles on the floor and the crème wallpaper with the French lilies in gold on it. She led them through to the great dining room where the living family was cramped with the ancestors. Some of them were half in and half out of the walls and the huge, honey-brown table and others were hovering around the living members, passing right through them in their jittery flowing. Good-natured curses were thrown around—having a ghost pass through you wasn't bad, just strange enough to make you wish you could scratch yourself on the inside—and all eyes were on them. Grann stepped between them, taking their hands.

"*Fanmi*, this is our new brother, Jon's mate, Barion." She held up Barion's hand like the referee in a boxing match, and the family cheered. Like a musician perfectly in tune with their instrument, Grann let the shouts go on for some time before she urged Jon and Barion toward two chairs in the middle of the long side of the table. With the sun streaming in from behind them, Jon knew they looked as if they were having a halo. It also put them in the middle of the family, many of whom started to sit down around the table while others hurried in the direction of the kitchen, no doubt getting all the food that the delicious scents permeating the house had promised. Grann sat down at the head of the table, overlooking the interrogation. Jon saw Amede and Gaspar hovering around her chair, their expressions too worried for the occasion. He decided to wait until after they had all eaten to find out what was going on.

"Hi, I'm Calixte, Amede's granddaughter. It's so nice to finally meet you, Barion. Can you tell me how many people you have killed?"

"Calixte!" Jon hissed, but she just smiled as if it were the most natural thing to inquire about a person's kill count right after meeting them for the first time. Next to him, Barion chuckled.

"Hi, Calixte. Nice to meet you too. Do you want the official version, the one I'm telling my father to keep him off my back, or the one I stick to when I'm with my brothers to look good?"

Calixte's eyes went wide for a moment. Barion had clearly managed to get her off balance. Then she tapped the long, bright yellow nail of her index finger against her lower lip. "I think I want the truth." She grinned, obviously thinking she had gotten Barion, but his perfect mate just laughed.

"There never is just one truth with demons, my dear. It's what makes us so unique."

"Nice escape, *demontre*. I'm Refoel, Gaspar's nephew, and my uncle wishes to know how you plan to make Jon happy?"

Jon shot a warning glare in Refoel's direction, which the man ignored completely. Gaspar came floating over, probably decoyed by the mention of his name. Barion leaned back in his chair, one hand casually on Jon's neck in a not-so-subtle show of ownership—Jon didn't mind, not at all, he *loved* it—the other stretched out in front of him. The demon stared at his nails while he pretended to think about the question.

"Well, I have the financial means to take care of Jon for the rest of our eternity together, if that's what you mean. As for the rest"—Barion looked at Jon so full of love that it almost hurt—"Jon is my mate. I'd do anything to make him happy. He wants to go to Hawaii for a day on the beach? Done. He wants me to cook for him? I know the best chefs in the world and my love for him runs so deep that I would never subject him to my cooking." That got Barion a round of happy laughter, indicating he was winning the tough crowd over. "He wants me to cuddle him because he had a bad day? I'm a demon. I can not only cuddle him, but I've also got a built-in heating blanket as well. He wants the moron who made him upset pay? I know dimensions where bodies disintegrate faster than you can say *wi*."

More laughter and an older woman named Edwige, a great-great-great-niece of Grann's, leaned over. "We may have need of that particular skill of yours, Barion."

"*Ase*, Edwige." Grann's voice was sharp like a whip, startling the three people coming through the doors with the first trays of food. The heavenly scent of Gumbo, fried pork chops and crawfish filled the room. Grann's fierce reaction, though, took Jon's focus from the food. He stared at her, then around the table, where he saw expressions carefully schooled to neutrality. A look at the hovering ancestors showed him concern bordering on fear. Something was very wrong, and there was no way Jon would be able to enjoy the family gathering — maybe 'enjoy' was too grand a word, more like not hate it — with something so sinister hovering over their heads.

"Grann, what are you not telling us?" Jon fixed her with what he hoped was a scalding look. From the corner of his eye, he saw Amede crossing his arms, huffing it out a bit for show, which totally ruined what little strictness Jon had managed to build up.

"*Wi*, Grann, why don't you tell Jon and his mate what is going on?" The other ancestors as well as the living family members had gone completely quiet. It was obviously unnerving, telling Jon how very serious the situation was. He felt his anxiety levels rise. Barion took his hand and squeezed it.

Grann shot Amede a scalding look and the spirit instantly vanished with a little shriek. Jon realized he still had a long way to go when it came to intimidation. Then again, he now had a demon as a mate. He guessed showing people their place was now Barion's job. Focusing back on his Grann, he saw a wary look on her face. She sighed and gestured for Jon to sit down again.

"Fine, I'm going to tell you. I didn't want to ruin your honeymoon, now that you're finally getting some."

"*Grann!*" Jon knew he would have been beet red if zombies could blush. Next to him, Barion was doing his best not to laugh. Needless to say, he wouldn't win any prizes for self-restraint any time soon.

"Oh, come on. I'm not blind, and your *demontre* is a hunky piece of sex candy."

"Eye candy, Grann. You mean eye candy. And stop trying to distract me."

Grann shrugged. "It was worth a try. Anyway, you see, there's this voodoo priest who has recently moved to New Orleans. He's from Haiti and an absolute asshole, dabbles in the blackest of magic. He's also like a rabid bear in front of a honey comb when it comes to power."

She didn't have to say more. Jon had seen enough challenges in his time with the Honoré family to know how this would end.

"He has challenged you."

Grann nodded.

"But you can beat him, can't you?" Barion sounded worried, picking up on Jon's anxiety through their mate bond. The family was still suspiciously quiet. The worried looks didn't help.

Grann gave a deep sigh. "I'm positive I can beat him. He may have given himself completely to the darkest sides of our *majik*, thus amassing more power than usual, but I've been around a lot longer than him. I know all the tricks in the book — and quite a few outside."

Jon furrowed his brows. "Then why are the ancestors so restless?"

"They sense he's going to do something really bad. They can't see more, and neither can I. It's all hazy."

"So, what's the plan?" Jon didn't really dare ask, but he had to know. He loved his Grann so much, and he couldn't even think about losing her.

"I go in with all I have, see what he's got and hope Papa Legba is still on my side."

"That's not exactly the glowing self-confidence I would have wished for."

"Unfortunately, it's all I have." For the first time since he'd met her, Grann looked her age. Jon felt an icy fist clenching his insides. Then Barion placed his hand on Jon's shoulder, the demonic warmth soothing him immediately.

"I'd say you've got a lot more," his mate said. "I'm a bit rusty on magical duels, but everything goes, doesn't it?"

Grann's gaze drilled into Barion. "Yes. Everything within the combatants' skill sets, which is usually the kind of *majik* they've learned, be it voodoo or hedge witchery or any of the other kinds."

"Then it's easy. You're going to summon one of the demon princes to squash that bug bothering you. It sends a strong signal to anybody contemplating challenging you for your crown, and I get to scare an idiot. Plus, Calixte can see me playing with a human firsthand." Barion grinned, showing his impressive teeth, the fangs just elongated enough to seem threatening. Calixte gave a little squeal, not at all intimidated or put off by the idea of watching a demon do...*things* with a human. Jon felt pride of his mate swelling up inside his chest, quickly followed by worry.

"Barion, what if something happens to you?"

Barion leaned toward him for a kiss. "I'm indestructible, remember? Whatever magic that roach is throwing at me, it won't harm me. And should he, for some impossible reason, be able to bind me, all you have to do is call Dre to kill him. Nobody can bind more than one demon at a time."

"You would do that for your Grann?" Grann asked before Jon could come up with other reasons why Barion shouldn't be taking such a risk, small as it was. Barion pulled Jon closer to his body.

"Of course I would. It's tradition to impress the in-laws."

Grann chuckled. "I like your *demontre*, Jon. He's a good man and worthy mate."

Under his cheek, Jon could feel Barion's chest puffing up. So much for a short, peaceful visit. The interrogation at the table seemed trivial all of a sudden. On the upside, the ancestors as well as the family members were now a lot friendlier toward Barion, presenting him with the best pieces of each dish, urging him to try everything and gushing to Jon what a good choice in a mate he had made, as if choice had had anything to do with it. Barion seemed to be happy, though, bathing in the admiration of his new relatives — there was no doubt he was adopted into the fold already — and pressing kisses to Jon's temple now and then. Jon tried to enjoy the food as well, not thinking too hard about everything that could go wrong during a freaking magical duel.

Chapter Sixteen

The next morning they were all up early, if not bright. At some point Grann had gotten the bourbon out, and Barion, never one to be shown up, had made a short trip to Scotland and his favorite distillery. Alcohol didn't work on zombies and demons but all-the-better on humans. Holding Calixte's hair while she lost everything she had consumed to the porcelain god was not Jon's idea of a fun-filled evening, and neither was stopping a stupidly drunk Refoel from pissing into the potted palm Grann had in her hall. The man had loudly insisted that it would do the plant good, his piss being a wonderful fertilizer, while Jon had feared the poor thing would wither and die when it came in contact with what had to be almost pure alcohol after the amounts of liquor the young man had guzzled. Edwige had insisted on Barion dancing with her, where she'd tried to climb him like a jungle gym, all the while screeching like a banshee about how men had to be conquered as if they were mountains. It only ended when she managed to reach Barion's shoulders, where she took one look at the floor way below her and fainted. Luckily for her, Barion had caught her before gently laying her on an antique chaise with upholstery in dark red brocade. Grann had cackled like a mad woman the entire time, the way she shot Barion warm looks when she thought nobody was aware of it the only indication how worried she had been about the duel.

After all the family members had passed out from alcohol consumption, Grann had sent them to bed in Jon's old room, which — to his utter mortification — was still the same way he had left it. It was complete chaos, the picture of a young Jason Momoa pinned to the ceiling above the bed and a life-sized Mr. Spock made from cardboard standing in one corner. Luckily for him, he had the best mate a zombie could wish for. Barion had pounced on Mr. Spock, doing the Vulcan greeting complete with *May you live long and prosper*, before he let himself fall on his back on the bed, staring up at Momoa in his *Stargate Atlantis* gear.

"Do you want to get naughty while Jason watches us?" Barion had winked, which had done wonderful things to Jon's lower body. Normally he would have balked at the idea of having sex under his Grann's roof, with the entire family gathered, but the living members were all knocked out from too much bourbon and whiskey, the ancestors watched him all the time anyway — it was amazing what a zombie could get used to when he regularly practiced the art of ignorance — and Grann? Well, Grann had buried more than one husband and lover, and probably knew more about sex than Jon cared to ever learn. They had given Jason Momoa quite the show — thrice, thank you very much — before falling asleep.

Now they were sitting at the table in the dining room with Grann, who was already dressed for the duel. She had taken out one of her favorite dresses, a red tunic, and had given her face what she called the full makeup treatment, meaning her eyes were surrounded by white paste with black and red dots, her lips painted a glossy ruby red and her cheeks highlighted with gold. On everybody else, this would have seemed as too much, but on Grann, the look worked. She was a badass voodoo priestess, and today, it showed in more than just the way she moved and talked and looked at people. She was sipping on her morning tea, spiked with the leftover bourbon from the previous night. Barion had brought crêpes from Paris and *Poffertjes* from Amsterdam. Fresh strawberries and cream made it all even better, even though nobody from the family seemed to be willing to eat with them. Edwige was still on the chaise, not moving a single muscle, and the house was quiet apart from a soft moan of pain here and there.

The duel was set for ten in the morning and by then, everybody would be on their feet, most probably wishing for death and swearing to never ever touch a drop of alcohol again. If everything worked as planned, those promises of sobriety would be forgotten in the evening when Grann's victory would be celebrated. Jon found the reliable behavioral patterns of his family more soothing than annoying, at least in this case. His own nerves were still wired, and not even the warmth of Barion's touch was able to calm him down.

"It's okay, Jon. Barion will make the bad man go away, won't you, *demontre*?" Grann smiled at Barion, who nodded with his mouth full of crêpe.

After he had swallowed, he said, "I've already texted Dre. He'll keep an ear open starting at ten. All you have to do is call him by his full name and infuse it with a bit of your power. He'll hear you and be there in a second, should what's-his-name have an ace up his sleeve I didn't see coming, though I highly doubt it."

"Don't jinx it." Jon touched Barion's arm, needing to feel his strength.

Barion turned his body fully to Jon and tugged him against his chest. "I don't. You won't lose me, *iubit*. I promise."

"Trust in fate, Jon. You wouldn't have gotten your mate just for him to be taken away again." Grann's voice was soft. She wasn't mocking him or disregarding his fear, unreasonable as it might be.

"I'm trying, okay?" He snuggled into Barion's embrace, basking in his warmth.

The conversation went to lighter topics, Barion telling Grann about his mansion in the Carpathians and what a struggle it had been to get the right wood for the floors. She could definitely relate, because keeping her own house in all its old grandeur wasn't an easy feat. Jon stayed in his mate's arms, his eyes half closed, listening to the soothing rhythm of their talk while the sun climbed higher in the sky and the family members slowly found their way to the table, all refusing the crêpes and *Poffertjes*, instead falling on the coffee as if dying from lack of caffeine was a thing.

At half past nine they got up to make their way to the old Holt Cemetery with its huge oaks guarding it. Barion offered to open a rift, but Grann didn't want to give her trump card away before it was necessary. She did have a flair for drama, her soul be blessed. In the end, they drove there in a long convoy, earning them odd looks from the tourists and bows from the locals. Barion was now fully glamoured and would stay with the cars until Grann called him. Jon didn't feel happy about parting with his mate but didn't want Grann to face the voodoo priest—his name was Fabien, as Jon had found out during the car ride—alone. Barion gave him a deep kiss and the promise to follow that up as soon as Fabien was dealt with. As a result, Jon was now anxious for two reasons.

Grann took his arm when they entered the cemetery, followed by the family, the ancestors hovering around them. Fabien was waiting under a particularly huge oak. Jon looked very closely at the man who thought challenging his Grann was a good idea. He was of average height, perhaps a few inches taller than Jon, and his skin was a deep black with a greyish tinge, something Jon had learned to recognize as a sign of heavy magic abuse, which told him the man wasn't powerful on his own merit but had to force the *majik*. That was never a good idea because magic didn't like to be forced where it didn't want to flow. Fabien had a voodoo stick in his hands and two pale men at his side, who had the empty look of mind slaves—another thing Jon had seen and learned to detest. Grann was strictly against it, because it was irreversible and the power necessary to keep the spell going was too huge to be trifled with. Fabien, it seemed, had no regard for rules or limits or decency. He was dressed in a tunic similar in cut to Grann's. Though where Grann's cloth was bright and cheery, Fabien was clad in black. He stared at them when they came closer, the slight widening of his eyes the only indication that he had realized what Jon was—or he was just surprised by how many people had come with Grann, or he had a sudden burst of stomach cramps or his eyes were simply twitchy. After all, it was no secret in the world of *majik* that Grann and Jon were blessed by Papa Legba.

"I thought you wouldn't show, *bouzen*," Fabien said with a sneer. Jon felt his hackles rise. Nobody talked to his Grann like that!

"And I thought a big bad voodoo priest like yourself would know better. Seems we were both mistaken." Grann remained absolutely calm and smiled brightly at Fabien, like what Jon thought a saber-tooth tiger would have looked like were it still alive. Fabien huffed, seemingly not knowing what to say for a moment. He soon found his arrogance again, which Jon thought was a shame.

"Fine. If you're that intent on dying, let's get on with it." He gestured at two circles scratched into the soft earth of the old cemetery. Jon assumed he had done that before their arrival. "As the challenged, I'll let you choose."

Grann shrugged. "It makes no difference to me." She stepped forward and into the circle closest to her. Fabien took his position in the other circle, watching the assembled crowd with a cold look. The family had no problem returning it with venom.

"Get ready to bow to your new king," he said. "Let's make this quick." He closed his eyes and started reciting something in Latin. With a sense of dread, Jon realized it was a demon summoning. He couldn't believe it. Fabien was trying to get a demon to do his bidding, and he didn't even bother with a proper summoning circle or any of the props. He just called the demon. Jon looked at his Grann, who was watching Fabien with narrowed eyes.

The voodoo priest finally got to the last line, "*Ego ut ad te oriuntur*, Corriwyn!" and Jon wasn't sure if the relieved sigh that wanted to leave his mouth was already called for. He was pretty sure Fabien had no real power over the demon he had just summoned, but one could never know. Jon watched as a rip in the fabric of space appeared and a demon with light gray scales and bronze markings stepped between the two rings. He looked positively scary. His claws were fully out, his impressive wings spread and his fangs were glistening in the sunlight. He towered over the assembled humans like the giant mammoth trees over their own saplings.

Fabien looked around the massive form at Grann, no doubt expecting her to be cowering in fear. "As I said, *bouzen*, let's make this quick. I have a city to get under my rule."

Grann just shrugged. "*Wi*, let's make this quick, *debutan*." She winked at Jon. "Barion, *cherie*, would you please come help your Grann out?"

At the name 'Barion', Corriwyn turned toward Grann, looking at her with interest before taking a step backward when another rip in the fabric of space appeared. Barion pushed through, grinning at the other demon.

"Uncle Corriwyn, so nice to meet you here!" Barion had his fangs in and his wings folded at his back. That didn't make him look any less threatening, though. Corriwyn obviously didn't mind. He smiled broadly, his fangs retreating as well while he opened his arms to hug Barion.

"Barion, I haven't seen you in ages! What are you doing here?"

"Corriwyn, *ego ut te occidere haec mulier!*" Fabien sounded a bit out of breath, probably due to the fact that he was realizing things were getting out of hand and not in his favor. He could as well have been one of those ridiculously small dogs that fit in a teacup, yapping at two Great Danes. The demons ignored him.

"Uh, you see, I've found my mate and the human you're playing with wants to kill his Grann."

"What? Congratulations. I haven't heard."

"It's very new, happened only two days ago. There will, of course, be an official announcement and party. Anyway, I can't let you kill Jon's Grann, seeing as she's my Grann now as well."

"Oh, that. It's fine. I wasn't planning on doing it, anyway. That idiot" — Corriwyn gestured at Fabien, who was getting quite red in the face — "has started summoning me about a month ago and he's been fun so far. But you know I draw the line at killing." He turned to Grann and bowed gracefully. "I'm truly sorry about the inconvenience, *bel leve*. If I had known this man was going to bother a woman of your beauty and grace, I would have never let him believe he could control me."

"It is fine, *bote nob*. You couldn't know. Let's put the blame where it belongs, won't we?" Grann patted her hair. She actually *patted* her hair, which she had adorned with two bird skulls and several feathers to mark the occasion, and now she was adjusting her breasts under her bright red silken tunic in a none-too-subtle way. Corriwyn was following her movements like a lion ready to pounce on the antelope. The very willing antelope, if Grann's blinding smile had anything to say.

"I told you to kill that freaking bitch, *move lespri!*" Fabien was shouting at the top of his lungs, waving around his stick with pearl beads, a small, hollowed pumpkin and three rat skulls attached to it. Jon was pretty sure that the man would blow a vessel any moment. Both Corriwyn and Barion slowly turned toward the enraged man, their eyes glowing deep red. It was Corriwyn who spoke.

"*Bel leve*, what do you want to happen to this worm?"

Grann stepped out of the circle and between the two demons, who towered over her like the world's most frightening bodyguards. "Well, he wanted me dead to take over my city and no doubt rule my people with fear and hate and disregard. He threatened my family. What does one do to such a person?" She tapped her chin with her right index finger.

Fabien seemed to have finally realized that he wouldn't win this fight, and he raised his stick, opening his mouth to start some recitation or other. Almost absent-mindedly, Barion grabbed the magical item and broke it in half. Fabien screeched and doubled over in pain. Jon didn't know much about the making of these kinds of sticks, because they were another thing Grann was strictly against, one of the reasons being that too much of the wielder flowed into the vessel, something Barion had just proven nicely with the unwilling help of Fabien. Corriwyn bent forward, grabbing Fabien at the collar of his silken—and no doubt expensive—tunic, lifting him into the air like the cockroach he was. The man started screaming, demanding to be let down, which Corriwyn ignored.

"I'm not sure how I want to deal with you," Corriwyn admitted. "Part of me wants to rip you apart and present the pieces to this lovely woman. The problem with that is, she'd be drenched in your blood, and while there are some who might find that hot, I'm not one of them."

"How thoughtful of you," Grann said. "I've yet to find something that really gets those pesky stains out."

Corriwyn smiled down at her. It was easy to see he was smitten. He had that same glazed-over look that Dre got every time Sammy's name was mentioned.

"Then what would you suggest?" he asked.

Grann grinned. "Well, he is a cockroach. Maybe, if he had to live life as one for, say, a year, he might learn manners. Ooh, or he could be a dung beetle. Imagine the fun he'd have in rolling balls of poo for a whole year!" She cackled.

Corriwyn chuckled. "You have an evil soul, my dear. I think you and I could have so much fun together."

Jon couldn't believe it. They were openly flirting. His Grann didn't flirt. She was his Grann! One look at Calixte, who made a face like she'd bitten into a lemon, told him she was as horrified as he was...or sick. She did look a bit green around the gills.

"Let me down, *move lespri!*" Fabien screeched, squirming in Corriwyn's grip like a worm on a hook. Corriwyn and Barion shared a look. Then Corriwyn turned to Grann.

"*Bel leve*, would you mind terribly if I dumped this rude piece of crap in another dimension? I know just the place. The rats there are huge." He winked.

"Then he should feel right at home, even though I'm afraid I'm insulting rats as a whole here." Grann did a courtesy...a freaking courtesy. "Do with him as you see fit, but return swiftly to my home so I can thank you properly, *bote nob*."

"It will be my pleasure, *bel leve*."

With his free hand, Corriwyn opened a rift and stepped through it. Barion stared at Grann. "I helped too, you know."

"I do, and you were great." Grann was looking at the two mind slaves who were still standing beneath the branches of the oak tree. She sighed. "Calixte, *cherie*, would you hand me my purse, please?"

When Calixte stepped forward, holding out Grann's purse—a leather monstrosity containing everything from candy wrappers to molten lip gloss to dried frogs and lost universes—Grann sighed even more deeply. She rummaged in the bag, finally pulling out a dagger. It had a bone handle and was made from flint, passed on from one generation of Honoré priests and priestesses to the next. Jon knew it was sharp enough to cut a hair in half. Grann waved Calixte away.

"It's better if you all leave now. This is priestess business."

The family immediately started filing out of the cemetery. Jon and Barion stayed behind, his mate not willing to leave him. Grann shot them an annoyed look. "I said leave."

"No." Jon crossed his arms, and Grann's eyes turned as hard as the flint of the knife.

"This isn't for you to see, Jon. You needn't know."

Jon let his arms drop. "I think I know what you're about to do," he said with a quick glance at the two slaves, who hadn't moved a muscle since the whole challenge had begun. "You shouldn't be doing it alone."

Grann's gaze softened. "It's the burden of the priestess, *cherie*. I know how to deal with it."

"Can't you just wait till the magic runs out?" Barion was looking at the two slaves. "It's already low. It can't take long."

"Oh, *demontre*, if only it were so easy." Grann looked at the knife in her hands. "You're right, of course, the magic is running out. Unfortunately, they won't get their minds back once Fabien's influence is gone. In order to enslave them, he had to kill the spirit inside. They will be like empty vessels waiting to be filled. That's no way to live." She looked at the two men with pity in her eyes. After a moment, the pity morphed into determination, and she gripped the handle of the knife harder. "If you must stay, do it, but don't interfere."

Jon felt Barion's hand on his shoulder. "We won't, Grann. And we won't leave you alone, either."

She smiled sadly. "*Merci.*"

Jon could feel Barion's nod more than he saw it from where his mate was standing slightly to his right. Grann started toward the two poor men. Before she could reach them, the flutter of wings cut through the air and a black cock with impressive spurs and a mean-looking beak landed on a branch of the oak where the slaves were standing. He cocked his head to the side, eyeing Grann with his huge eyes. Papa Legba's voice resounded inside their heads.

"This is not a burden you have to shoulder today, my priestess."

He fluttered into the air, a little less impressive than when he had flown into the cemetery, because he was only going a short way. Papa Legba landed on the shoulder of the first man, touching his beak to his temple. The man gave a sigh before his body went lax.

Papa Legba had to do some frantic fluttering to stay in the air. He then landed on the other man's shoulder, doing the same to him. Jon could feel that both men were dead. Released. Grann bowed to the cock who had flown back to the branch.

"Thank you, Papa Legba."

"You're most welcome." The bird turned his head toward Barion. "And thank you for aiding my priestess. That man has been a thorn in my side for some time now."

Barion nodded. "I have to thank you, Papa Legba, for bringing Jon back."

The cock rustled his feathers. "That was the Norns. Well, it was *me* who brought him back, but on the insistence of the Norns."

"I'm grateful anyway." Barion winked.

"Would you have wanted Fabien for yourself?" Grann seemed a bit worried.

The cock shook his head so fiercely that his cock's comb was slapping against the sides of his neck. "No, wherever your demon friend is taking him is perfect. He cannot pass back into this realm. That's all that counts for me. I don't want to deal with a soul as black as his. They usually turn into something nasty upon death."

"Well, he's not going to make it long where Corriwyn is dumping him, but I doubt the rats will be overly impressed by whatever he turns into."

As if Barion's words had summoned him, a rift appeared in the fabric of space and Corriwyn stepped through. He looked around until his gaze found Grann.

"*Bel leve*, it is done. This man will never bother you again." He bowed elegantly then gave the cock a short salute. "Papa Legba. Long time no see."

"I'm happy as well." The cock flustered his feathers. Jon thought he detected a hint of sarcasm but decided he wasn't fluent enough in avian-god to read anything into it.

Corriwyn stepped next to Grann, offering her his arm. "*Bel leve*, how about we leave this place and I'll show you one of the best cafés in France?"

Grann giggled, and Jon was fluent enough in female to know she was flirting like crazy. "Oh, *bote nob*, it would be my pleasure, but I think I need a change of dress." She gestured at herself. Corriwyn shook his head as if he were horrified.

"No, no, *bel leve*, there is no need for changing. First of all, you're more than perfect the way you are, I absolutely adore powerful women, and secondly, I would never take you to a place where you wouldn't be welcome in any way, shape or form you choose."

"He's taking her to the Café Le Enfers. It's run by a clan of vampires." Barion whispered in Jon's ear.

"Vampires!" Jon shook his head.

"Don't worry. They're like Emilia — business before pleasure and all that. Plus, you're Grann is absolutely capable of taking care of herself, and with Corriwyn around, nothing can happen."

"That's what *you* say."

"It's not as if you could stop them," Barion pointed out.

"Ahem, I have to ask this." Papa Legba had flustered his feathers until he looked twice as big, staring at Corriwyn with his beady eyes. "What are your intentions with *my* priestess?"

"My intention is to woo this gracious example of perfect female beauty until she agrees to let me give her whatever her heart desires." Corriwyn winked and

Papa Legba lifted one of his legs, showing off his spores in silent warning.

Grann was holding onto Corriwyn's arm with one hand while stroking his biceps with the other. It was obvious what plans she had with the demon, and Jon wished his imagination weren't as lively as it was or he would die a quick death. Such was his luck that neither happened and he had the great pleasure of watching a silent stare off between Corriwyn and Papa Legba until Grann got impatient, told her god goodbye and ordered Corriwyn to get going, which the demon immediately did. When they were gone, Papa Legba made a clucking sound before he gave a long and loud cock's crow. He jumped down from the oak to land between the bodies of the two mind slaves. For a moment, Jon's vision blurred. When it cleared again, Papa Legba and the corpses were gone.

"What an interesting visit," Barion commented dryly.

"Was Corriwyn serious? About giving Grann whatever she wants?"

"*Iubit*, I think it's best not to think about what these two are going to do. Let's just assume they're going to have fun and leave it at that." Barion sounded almost desperate.

"Your wisdom matches your years, mate of mine." Jon winked.

Barion huffed in mock irritation and grabbed Jon around the waist. "Years, my ass. I'll show you years."

He lifted his hand to open a rift. "Wait! Before we go home, we need to get back to Grann's house and tell the others everything is fine." Jon didn't look forward to dealing with a bunch of agitated humans and even more spirits, but what choice did he have? Somebody had to smooth everything over.

Barion sighed. "Fine. Just let me stress that it was *your* idea, not mine."

"Yeah, yeah, I take full responsibility. Now let's get it done."

Chapter Seventeen

Telling Jon's family that Grann was hopping around the world with a demonic suitor went down about as well as Barion had feared. The ancestors hadn't been able to track her because they had still been gathered at the house with the rest of the family waiting for her return when Grann had decided it was time for her to enjoy a third or fourth spring with Corriwyn.

"I'm sure she'll be back soon." Jon tried to raise his voice over the hubbub of murmuring in the dining room. "You can all go back home, get some sleep, lose those headaches you surely have after all the alcohol and excitement, and before you know it, everything will be back to normal."

"Sleep sounds good." Calixte pressed her fingers against her temples. "I think I'll take some aspirin and try to forget the image of Grann flirting with a nine-foot demon. Yes, yes, that's what I'm going to do."

She turned toward the main door, the rest of the family following her.

"He's only eight feet. In fact, he's a little smaller than me." Barion felt it was necessary to make that clear. Jon took his hand and kissed the back of it.

"I know you're bigger than him, my sweet demon."

Barion decided to ignore the hint of laughter in Jon's voice. His mate was under a lot of stress what with introducing Barion to the family, the magical duel and now Grann hooking up with Corriwyn. There, he'd said it. Grann was hooking up with his great-uncle. She had every right to do so. She was a woman in her…prime—*yes, in her prime*—and Corriwyn was a suitable…fitting…tolerable…barely worthy candidate. It was all good, and they needed to get home so he could watch some Iron Bull and pray to forget what he had seen.

Barion prided himself on being the epitome of tolerance when it came to the different shapes relationships could take, but Grann was Jon's grandmother, a respected and respectable voodoo priestess of a certain age, and the image of her and Corriwyn doing…*things* was too strange for Barion's mind to comprehend. Then a picture of Mavis and Maribel appeared in his mind's eye, along with some of the naughtier things they used to say, and all of a sudden he could be happy for Grann…*mostly*.

"Think of Mavis and Maribel," Barion whispered into Jon's ear. His gorgeous mate sighed.

"You're right, but this is my *Grann*." He shrugged. "Well, I guess, I'll survive. Let's go home?"

"Let's go home. We have a video call tomorrow with Endless Horizon and need to be prepared."

Jon snuggled under Barion's arm, his favorite place to hop through space, as Barion knew by now. They arrived back at Jon's place and had exactly five minutes to themselves before the bell rang. Jon groaned.

"I'm coming." He opened the door for Dre, Sammy and the rest of the book club, who all filed into the apartment without hesitation. Amber and Emilia hugged Jon while Declan and Troy went straight for Barion, to give him appreciative pats on the shoulder.

"Congratulations, man. We're so happy for you two!" Declan grinned broadly.

"Yeah, who would have thought Jon and you are mates?" Troy looked at Jon, who was at that moment getting a close-up view of Maribel's bosom. Mavis was saying something that had Sammy, who was standing next to them, blushing fiercely.

"Thank you. And to be honest, if I had taken one moment to really think about everything, I should have realized what was going on."

"Ah, don't be too hard on yourself, man. Jon has no scent, so you didn't have the slightest clue what he could be to you." Troy made a show of sniffing the air. "Though now he seems to have gotten a scent of his own. It's a mixture of you and…truffles? With rum?"

Declan held up his nose as well. "Yeah. Truffles and rum."

"I'm not sure I like you sniffing out my mate. And I" — Barion took a deep breath as well — "smell sun and cream and blackberries, thank you very much."

Declan shrugged. "Scent is always different for mates." He and Troy went to congratulate Jon while Amber, Emilia and the witches descended on him.

Amber hugged his waist, not able to reach any higher, while Emilia simply floated up a bit to give him a kiss on each cheek. Mavis and Maribel grabbed his arms and tugged him down to get their arms around his neck, a chance Amber apparently didn't want to miss, because she dove into the hug again. After the initial round of congrats, it was an impromptu party with food Dre and the witches provided. Barion had to admit that it was nice, celebrating with their family and friends.

"Oh, I almost forgot... Dad and Quirion send their love. They're looking forward to the official party." Sammy took a huge spoonful of crème brûlée, moaning at the taste. Dre was eyeing his mate like *he* was some kind of delicious dessert.

"Where is Dad? I know Quirion won't come out of his library under any circumstances, but I thought he would be here."

"Dad had to go to that weird dimension where gravity is spotty. You remember that one?" Dre had one hand on Sammy's shoulder, gently massaging his mate's neck with his thumb.

"Yeah, you never know when you're going to fly and when you're dropping like a rock. It's fun." Barion had fond memories of that particular dimension. It probably wouldn't be as nice without the incubus who had visited it with him back in. *Damn, back in the seventeenth century.* It was something he wouldn't mention to Jon, who was currently talking animatedly to Mavis and Amber, though he could see himself and Jon visiting there soon. The possibilities were endless. "What's going on there?"

Sammy huffed. "Friendly family strategy game gone awry."

"Oh." Barion could imagine the carnage. "How many players?"

"Twenty." Dre winced.

"Damn. That's a violation of the first rule." Barion shuddered.

"What's the first rule?" Jon had come over and snuggled under Barion's arm.

"Every gathering with more than five demons present is considered an attempt at war and therefore forbidden unless there's express permission from the king." Barion tugged Jon closer to his side.

"Judging from your looks, permission wasn't given?"

"No. Dad is furious." Dre grinned. "By the way, Jon, I think something has changed about your scent."

"Huh?" Jon looked up from where he was cuddled against Barion. "I don't have a scent."

"You have one now," Barion smiled at his mate full of love. "Troy and Declan have mentioned it as well. They say you smell of me, truffles and rum. To me, you smell of sun and cream and blackberries."

Dre sniffed the air, obviously thinking he was being discreet. "I'll have to second the werewolves. It's truffles and rum. I think I'm getting hungry."

Sammy held up a spoonful of his dessert to his mate. "Oh, *mo grah thu*, you take such good care of me."

"Only the best for my beloved mate."

Instead of feeling the green monster clawing at his insides, Barion could now watch his brother and brother-in-law with the happiness for them that they deserved.

"Could we go back to why I suddenly seem to have a scent?" Jon had lifted his arm and was sniffing his pit. It was so cute that Barion could have eaten him on the spot.

Barion threw his brother a questioning glance. "Any ideas?"

"Nope. My knowledge about zombies begins and ends with *The Walking Dead*. I'm sure it's not a reliable source, though we can always ask Quirion."

They both shuddered. "*Or* we could just accept it as the miracle and blessing it is and not bother the cranky hoarder of books in his cave." Barion winked.

"Since when does Quirion live in a cave?" Sammy seemed confused.

"He doesn't, *mo grah thu*, but you have to admit that his library kind of is his cave."

"Oh, now I get it. You're right, Dre." Sammy addressed Jon. "As long as the scent is pleasant, I wouldn't stress about it."

"Sound advice." Jon smiled. "You said you could perhaps help us with the official announcement party. Is that offer still on the table?"

Sammy clapped his hands. "Of course it is! I've already made a list of possible locations, and we need to talk food, and drinks, and do you want a florist?"

"Uhm, let's start with the location?" Jon squeezed Barion's hand. "What do you think, my mate?"

My mate. It was the sweetest sound in all the dimensions. And it was directed at him! Barion leaned to give his mate a kiss and everything he wanted.

Epilogue

Jon stood next to his gorgeous demon and welcomed their guests. It had been two weeks since his Grann had been challenged and so much had happened that his head was still spinning. After their initial brainstorming at the impromptu party with the book club, Jon had left the planning of the announcement party in Sammy's capable hands. His friend and landlord had outdone himself, only bothering Jon and Barion when there were important decisions to make, like should they have the party at Barion's mansion in the Carpathians or at Waaseyaa's place in Canada. Waaseyaa had cinched the deal by offering to have her famous pancakes coming the entire afternoon and evening. The weather was perfect — sunshine, but not too hot, with a few last patches of snow here and there and the air filled with birds' song.

With Sammy taking care of everything, Jon and Barion had had the time to close the deal with Jim Dalton and Annabelle Lee from Endless Horizon. *Demon Wars* would become the next big game in the company's portfolio, and Jon and Barion had full creative freedom backed by the knowledge and experience of several senior programmers at the company. They worked on the game day and night, sketching demons, designing levels, building the world and the story, and not one second of it was what Jon considered tedious. He got to do what he loved with the demon of his life, and things couldn't be more perfect if they were starring in a rom-com. The discussions about how to do certain things — well, to be honest, how to do *everything* — were passionate and always led to things that had little to do with the game. They were seriously considering including several romances in the game, using Iron Bull as their inspiration. They had to watch him and his Kadan a lot to make sure they truly understood everything. Life was sweet.

The book club was already in full attendance, even Declan and Troy had been able to be here from the start, not like at Sammy's and Dre's announcement party, where they had come late due to some business that had gone sideways. The two werewolves never talked much about what they did exactly, and Jon had the suspicion that not all their business trips were related to their official company. But they were powerful predators and perfectly capable of taking care of themselves — or so he hoped. Currently they were stuffing their faces with Waaseyaa's pancakes, praising the woman to the high heavens, which she soaked up like a dried-out sponge. The flirting was casual, as it always was with the two alphas, and Mavis and Maribel were there as well, keeping an eye on things.

Quirion was standing at the edge of the clearing behind Waaseyaa's diner, talking to Milo, who was hanging on his every word. Contrary to what Barion and Dre had anticipated — that Milo would either quit after the first month working for Quirion or ask for an outrageous amount of money to stay with their brother, which they had hoped for in order to help him and his mother out — the young man seemed to be getting along with the huge demon just fine after the initial shock of getting acquainted with Quirion's ways. Milo's mother was doing better, her surgery was scheduled for the next month and the doctors were more than optimistic that she would make a full recovery.

The air between two of the gigantic maple trees that marked the gateway into the forest and — for the initiated, as Jon had learned — to the spirit world, started shimmering. The ancestors appeared, led by Amede and Gaspar. They floated into the clearing, greeting people and waving at Jon. A rip appeared in thin air, through which Grann and Corriwyn stepped, followed by the family. A perfect gentleman, Corriwyn lent Grann his arm to step over the roots of the trees and onto the soft, fresh grass of the clearing. She wore a bright yellow and orange tunic, her hair was done up in a complicated braid adorned with a fake sunflower and a crow's skull. From her generous cleavage the runes marking her as Corriwyn's mate snaked their way up to her neck.

Jon couldn't say he had been surprised to learn that the two were mates, as well. The sparks flying between them could have ignited a soggy piece of loam. What had surprised him was how little time Grann and her *bote nob* had wasted on becoming mates. According to a shuddering Calixte, who had had the misfortune of walking into the house while they had worked up to the bite, it had happened two days after the challenge. And it had only *"taken so long"* —Grann's words, not his—because they had partied so hard at the club attached to the vampire café in Paris that they had forgotten the time. The important thing was that Grann was happy, Corriwyn was happy, the family and the ancestors were weirded out by the insane amount of sex Grann was having but happy, and therefore they had left Jon and Barion mostly to their own devices. It was a win-win situation if Jon had ever seen one.

Grann and Corriwyn came over to them and there were hugs and smiles. Then Grann went to talk to Waaseyaa, Mavis and Maribel. The four witches greeted each other warmly and even Jon, who wasn't good at detecting magic, could sense the power emanating from them.

Corriwyn stared in the direction of the women and sighed happily. "Isn't she gorgeous? And so much power. Makes me horny as fuck."

Barion chuckled. "To be honest, I would give them a wide berth. These four are trouble."

"Only in the best way. How are you two doing? The party looks nice."

"Sammy did most of it...thankfully. And we're doing great, aren't we, *iubit?*" Barion pressed a kiss to Jon's temple, making the skin tingle. He smiled up at his mate.

"We're perfect. Thank you for asking, Gramps."

Corriwyn winced. "I'm still not sure what to make of that title. I'm used to being dreaded, not some family figure."

"You're mated to my Grann, so that makes you 'Gramps'. Sorry."

"Don't be. I like it. It's just unfamiliar. Speaking of family, where's Alerion?"

Barion sighed. "He'll be here shortly. There was another forbidden gathering. I have a feeling some demons are getting restless."

"They should all find their mates. Then they'd be occupied with more important things." Corriwyn was staring at Grann again.

"Go over there. We're not holding you back. When's your and Grann's announcement party, by the way?" Barion plucked a neatly cut egg and ham sandwich from the table standing next to them.

"On the full moon after the one in two days. It will be a midnight party." Listening to the happiness in Corriwyn's voice, the party could have been at two in the morning on a glacier and he still would have been over the moon.

"Oh, I love midnight parties." Sammy stepped toward them with Dre in tow. He slung his arms around Corriwyn's waist.

"I'm so happy you found your mate, Uncle."

Corriwyn patted Sammy's back. "Thank you, little one."

"I heard there was a party?" Alerion's voice sounded right behind them. Jon turned with a huge smile on his lips.

"Dad, welcome! I'm so happy you're here." And Jon really was. Alerion was the kind of father he had always wished for and having to share him with Sammy made the whole family-sibling experience even better.

Alerion stepped forward to greet his sons and Corriwyn when suddenly there was a light breeze tousling their hair, followed by a rabid growl vibrating across the clearing. Declan and Troy were stalking toward Alerion, their eyes glowing in the deep amber that only alpha werewolves had.

"Mate!" they garbled through too-long fangs, shoving aside Dre and Corriwyn, who were standing in their way. Before anybody could react, they pounced on Alerion and brought him down, sniffing his neck like addicts a fresh tube of glue.

"Well, fuck me sideways," Barion announced to no one in particular.

Want to see more from this author? Here's a taster for you to enjoy!

Demon Mates: Demon's Dance
Xenia Melzer

Excerpt

Alerion, King of all Demons, the Mighty Warrior, Defeater of the Unruly, was flat on his back somewhere in a clearing in Canada, trying to comprehend what had just happened. There had been two growls, the nuance less threatening and more possessive, then a dual *"ours"*, followed by two muscular bodies barreling into him. As he had just been talking to his favorite son Sammy — although he had a feeling Jon would soon join Sammy on that pedestal — the attack had taken him by surprise.

It was hard to hear anything over the excessive sniffing taking place on both sides of his neck, but from what he could discern, people were rather more amused than worried. From somewhere, a *"Well, fuck me sideways!"* drifted to his ears, of no real consequence because the scent enveloping him — raspberries and cream with an undertone of cinnamon and clove — was way too pleasant to be thinking about anything else. The declarations of *"Mate!"*, *"Ours!"* and *"Claim!"* left him in no doubt as to what was happening.

I'm so lucky my mates are shifters! Otherwise, it would be the same back and forth that his sons Dre and Barion had had with their mates, and Alerion knew he could do without that drama in his life. In fact, ruling all demonkind was a drama in and of itself, which was why he tried to avoid it in all other aspects of his life — not that there was so much going on aside from cowing unruly demons and patiently explaining for the three-millionth time how nobody was as sturdy as a demon and, therefore, playing with other species — humans in particular — was forbidden. Nobody could accuse demons of being quick on the uptake.

"Uhm, Declan? Troy? Could you perhaps let Dad up?" Of course it was Sammy, the best son-in-law a demon king could wish for, who tried to end the spectacle. Alerion was of two minds about the sniffing ending because yes, getting to see his mates would be nice, no doubt, but on the other hand, it was also *very* nice to be so close to them.

"I'm not sure they can hear you, Sammy dear." *One of the witches...Mavis or Maribell.* Alerion didn't know them well enough to recognize by voice alone.

"Why do I have the sudden urge to bare my neck?" Jon, on the other hand, was easy to pick out.

"You're not baring your neck to anybody but me." *Barion, growling like a lion defending a fresh kill.*

"I didn't say I would do it — just that I have the feeling I should." Jon sounded part wounded, part soothing.

"What are we baring and why? Is this some custom nobody has told me about?" *Amber, the banshee,* Alerion thought. Her voice was quite distinctive, the screech to warn heroes of their impending death always present as an undertone. Most people couldn't discern it and just found Banshees' voices a bit unnerving, but Alerion wasn't most people.

"Well, I'm always up for a little baring of body parts." That voice sounded adventurous. It had to be

Corrywin's mate, Jon's Grann, the Voodoo priestess. Interesting woman and a perfect fit for his restless uncle.

"As much as I love all your body parts, *ma chere*, I think we should be helping Alerion first." *Corrywin, helpful as always. Not.*

"I thought we had to get naked?" *Amber again.*

"Nobody is baring anything!" Dre, his second oldest son, the lucky bastard who'd snatched Sammy.

"Can somebody explain to me what's going on?" Judging from the harmonious sound, it had to be Emilia, the vampire. Alerion liked her because she was very down-to-earth, despite her royal ancestry.

"It's simple, dear." *One of the witches.* "Declan and Troy have finally found their third, and in their exuberance, they have forgotten not only their manners but also to shield their auras, which can be overwhelming since they are uber alphas—hence the urge to show submission. Declan! Troy! Stop with the sniffing and get up. Your mate must be uncomfortable with both of you pinning him down."

The last sentences were said with a scolding undertone of 'bad boys!', which caused the sniffing to stop. Alerion bemoaned this for about half a second before he realized he was now free to admire his mates.

"What's an uber alpha?" *Sammy again, always eager to learn.* What a smart son he had gained!

Again, it was one of the witches answering. "Uber alphas are very rare. The last one was born some two hundred fifty years ago. They are so powerful all shifters immediately unite under them, which inevitably leads to bloody war. One prime example is Napoleon Bonaparte, the French emperor. He was the last uber alpha we knew of until Declan and Troy came along."

"Wow. Are you planning to do that any time soon? It's just that war is such a waste of lives and time." Sammy was addressing Alerion's mates, who had lifted their heads enough to stare at Sammy, which in turn gave Alerion a wonderful view of their breathtaking profiles. One of them was blond, the other's hair showed a rich dark brown, their noses were sharp, their jaws like carved from marble and their skin flawless perfection.

"Sammy, we're having a moment here!" The blond whined, his hands still resting on Alerion's chest, which he didn't mind at all.

"I can see that, Declan, but you have to admit that impending war is kind of a serious topic."

So, his blond mate was Declan — which meant the dark-haired one had to be Troy, who was the next to speak. "Sammy, how long do you know us? Three years? Four? Have you ever gotten the impression we would strive for world domination?"

Through the space between his mates' faces, Alerion could see Sammy furrowing his brows. *My son is a such a thinker! And my mates are so gorgeous!*

"Well, you're certainly rich enough to buy large parts of it." *Emilia, matter-of-factly.*

"Says the vampire with the *very* old money." *Amber, also winking.*

"So you don't want to wage bloody war?" Sammy sounded so happy.

"No." Declan sighed. "We don't like messes, remember?"

"Uh, almost forgot that. Well, a battlefield certainly isn't the place for somebody who dusts the *undersides* of their windowsills." Emilia grinned. "A trait I deeply admire."

"Because you completely lack it?" Troy raised the brow Alerion could see from his place on the ground. It almost made him swoon. *So beautiful.*

"I guess a battlefield is kind of messy—and unsanitary." Jon seemed to be deeply in thought.

"If you wanted to conquer the world, you would tell us, wouldn't you?" Amber sounded suspicious.

"Nobody is conquering anything—or waging bloody war or buying the world! All Declan and I want is to get our mate somewhere quiet with a nice big bed—emphasis on quiet. If you would excuse us?" Troy gracefully got up, offering Alerion his hand. Declan was on his feet as well, staring at Alerion as if he were a bloody steak and Declan starved. It was nice to be looked at with such hunger. Alerion felt his cock, which had been hard since the moment his mates had tackled him to the ground, twitching.

"Yes, I think a quiet place would be nice. How about we visit my little cabin in Whitewater where we can…proceed." Alerion had tried for subtlety and obviously failed spectacularly, given how everybody gathered around them was snickering. The two witches, Mavis and Maribell, seemed to be having their own little film going on in their heads while Grann was shamelessly making out with Corrywin. Sammy stared at them with big eyes—he was still so innocent, bless his sweetness—while Jon smiled at them encouragingly.

"Yes, let's proceed." Troy winked.

Both alphas were still holding Alerion's hands, and he tried to decide which one he should let go of to slice space and time when Dre stepped forward with a long-suffering sigh, solved this terrible conundrum by doing the slicing for him—he, too, was a good son and had brought Sammy into the family after all—and nodded at him. "Have fun, Dad. And congratulations. Declan, Troy. Congratulations to you as well. If you hurt my dad—"

"Yeah, yeah, you will do to us what we will do to you and Barion if you hurt Sammy or Jon." Declan was already stepping toward the slice.

"I just wanted to have it out in the open."

"It is. Bye. Enjoy the party." Troy was following his mate, tugging Alerion along. He knew his smile had to be showing all his teeth, but he was on his way to mate with the two most gorgeous creatures that had ever lived!

"Dre, thank you. Barion, Jon, I'm sorry I'm leaving so soon. I'm going to invite you to dinner. Promise. Sammy, don't worry."

They all waved, Jon saying something along the lines of "Finding your mate is the most important thing!" while Sammy was furiously wiping away his tears and simultaneously smiling so hard that his cheeks had to hurt.

"Congratulations, Dad, and have fun! You too, Declan, Troy."

"See you next Wednesday!"

Alerion stepped into the slice in space still holding the hands of both his mates. This day was certainly one to be remembered.

About the Author

Xenia Melzer was born and raised in a small village in the South of Bavaria. As one of nature's true chocoholics, she's always in search of the perfect chocolate experience. So far, she's had about a dozen truly remarkable ones. Despite having been in close proximity to the mountains all her life, she has never understood why so many people think snow sports are fun. There are neither chocolate nor horses involved and it's cold by definition, so where's the sense? She does not like beer either and has never been to the Oktoberfest – no quality chocolate there.

Even though her mind is preoccupied with various stories most of the time, Xenia has managed to get through school and university with surprisingly good grades. Right after school she met her one true love who showed her that reality is capable of producing some truly amazing love stories itself.

While she was having her two children, she started writing down the most persistent stories in her head as a way of relieving mommy-related stress symptoms. As it turned out, the stress-relief has now become a source of the same, albeit a positive one.

When she's not writing, she translates the stories of other authors into German, enjoys riding and running, spending time with her kids, and dancing with her husband.

Xenia loves to hear from readers. You can find her contact information, website details and author profile page at https://www.pride-publishing.com

PUBLISHING

Sign up for our newsletter and find out about all our romance book releases, eBook sales and promotions, sneak peeks and FREE romance books!